THE WELCOMING COMMITTEE

Traveler didn't like the looks of the wrecked truck up ahead. It was lying on its side, wheels facing away, blocking the road. There was something about it.

It was intact. And yet the skeleton in the cab made it look like it had been there for a long time. Somebody wanted it to look that way. Because it was a trap.

He pulled up short. Immediately the savages who'd been hiding behind the truck sprang into the open, weapons in hand. They were nude except for man-hide loincloths and vests decorated with strings of man-teeth and dried fingers. Their white skin was brightly painted in red and blue lightning patterns, their hair teased up and lacquered into shape, so that each man's coif resembled a nuclear bomb explosion. They were permanently stoned on smash-weed, and they came on like a pack of rabid dogs. . . .

Coming Soon

TRAVELER #3

THE STALKERS

by D. B. Drumm

Fifteen years after doomsday, survival is a vicious game. Nobody plays it better than the man called Traveler—nobody except the men who call themselves the Stalkers.

And be sure to watch out for the other Dell action series

THE BLACK BERETS

by Mike McCray

They learned their lethal skills on the secret battlefields of Vietnam. Now, they're fighting for themselves and not even the government can stop them.

HAWKER

by Carl Ramm

America's deadliest vigilante, he lives outside the law— to battle the forces no law can touch.

TRAVELER #2

KINGDOM COME

D. B. Drumm

A DELL BOOK

Published by
Dell Publishing Co., Inc.
1 Dag Hammarskjold Plaza
New York, New York 10017

Copyright © 1984 by Dell Publishing Co., Inc.

All rights reserved. No part of this book may be reproduced
or transmitted in any form or by any means, electronic or
mechanical, including photocopying, recording, or by any
information storage and retrieval system, without the written
permission of the Publisher, except where permitted by law.

Dell ® TM 681510, Dell Publishing Co., Inc.

ISBN: 0-440-14559-7

Printed in the United States of America

First printing—July 1984

Prologue

He was all alone on the road.

Just him and the sleek black van he drove. Just him and his ghosts.

He was driving through a sulfur-yellow wasteland, on a broken-backed road, and through the warm side of the year 2004 A.D. in what had, before the war, been the United States. Had been Kansas. Kansas was a fading memory. We're not in Kansas, Toto, no. Because there isn't one anymore.

He was in his late thirties, this lone man. He was neither tall nor short, neither thick nor thin. But he was strong, with a strength that came from within, a strength hinted at in the set of his strong jaw and the cold depth of his steely blue eyes. He was wearing combat boots and standard army fatigues, a sleeveless undershirt beneath his sleeveless black flak jacket. His brown hair was clipped short, almost punkishly bristly.

It was getting near noon when he saw the men on the motorcycles circling their victims by the roadside. He glimpsed a woman and terrified young men among the victims. He foresaw murder, and he shrugged. He kept driving.

1

Dark Knights on the Road

The man called Traveler was used to seeing murder by the roadside; he was used to seeing men prey on other men, and on women and children. The road, the highway, the freeway, was sort of an infinite version of the House Of Horror carnival rides he'd taken as a kid—only, out here in the Great Wastelands that had been the American Midwest, the blood wasn't painted on, and the knives weren't rubber.

Normally, he just kept on driving, no matter what he saw—unless he thought intervening might turn him a profit. He was working hard at burning out feelings of pity, of empathy.

But it seemed he hadn't quite succeeded. Because when he got a quarter mile past the melee on the roadside, the dust-clouded place where a band of motor-cycle thugs attacked a caravan, he gritted his teeth—and stopped. "You dumb son-of-a-bitch," he told himself. "Don't do it."

But he turned the car around and went back.

Okay, so maybe there'd be profit in it. Not likely. But maybe.

It was a hot day, windless, and dead at noon, the sun shining its merciless benediction down on the carnage. The highway cut straight through the new postwar dust bowl, like a weathered black snake hide stretched between two nails on the hoop of the horizon. It was pocked with potholes, every so often half-blocked with rusting wreckage.

The raw yellow-dust plains to either side were stubbled with scrub, boulders, and the occasional ruin. That was all.

Traveler leaned on the accelerator. He was driving a black, sleek, and badly scarred four-wheel-drive mini-van powered by one of the last Wankel universal engines produced in America. The windows were reinforced with iron shutters; the interior was lined with scrap iron and a half-dozen bulletproof vests he'd looted from an armory up north. From the same armory—guarded by the skeletons of four National Guardsmen who died in one of the many ways available in the days after the Blast—he had taken a Heckler and Koch HK91 heavy assault rifle, an Armalite AR-180 light assault rifle, a government-issue Colt .45 and a Remington 870 12-gauge shotgun. A few weeks back he'd picked up two HK21 light machine guns from what must have been a very high dollar survivalist reservation—too bad the plague had gotten them.

Traveler had bolted both the HK21's to the roof of the van's cab and streamlined them with a couple of fiber glass pods. The 7.62 chatterboxes were set so they pointed inward and slightly downward, their lines of fire converging about forty feet ahead of the van and four feet off the ground. He'd rigged them so they fired when he squeezed a homemade Fire button taped to the steering column. He had maybe four drums of 7.62-mm for the machine guns and two clips apiece for the assault rifles. The right ammo for a particular weapon was hard to come by; sometimes he had to make do with whatever he could scrounge. Luckily, he saved his brass, and as long as he could find enough wheel weights and print shop lead, he could cast his own slugs. He also had an unprimed lump of C4 that he kept around for the odd emergency.

The dust cloud to the left of the road grew more transparent as he got near, and through its yellow swirl he could make out about thirteen bikers ripping up the ground on low-slung hawgs, some three-wheelers, some deucies, circling three horse-drawn station wagons. The station wagons had had their engines torn out. The scarecrow horses reared and bucked with terror as the circle of howling bikers moved in closer. The three cars were arranged in a rough triangle, and the bikers circled them like Indians around covered wagons. As he passed the melee, his van jouncing as it hit a pothole, he checked out the enemy and the layout, beginning to form a rough plan. He swerved around an overturned semi-truck cab and cut abruptly to the left, popping the gears into four-wheel-drive to grind cross-country. Sage and the occasional stunted tree whipped past him; boulders loomed up and seemed to leap to one side as he snapped the power steering to avoid them, and then he was in a cloud of yellow, bearing down on the bikers.

The settlers from the caravan—or so he took them to be—were posted inside the triangle of steel and horse-flesh, firing what were probably their last few precious rounds of ammo at the bikers, to no noticeable effect. The big choppers roared and threw off shards of sunlight in the places where the dust cloud had cleared a little. One of them had snagged a teenaged boy with a noose around his ankle, dragging him screaming through the rocks, making hamburger out of him. A horse went down, shot through the neck, spurting an arc of blood; a handlebar-mounted crossbow shot a steel bolt into the tight knot of men crouched between the cars, catching a thickset middle-aged man in the gut. He fell, face contorted, writhing. Another bike was leaping from a fortuitous ramp of dirt and stones to land in the center of the triangle, his Harley bouncing, then fanning dust as it leaned over to circle back and ram through three of the men, the spikes on its handlebars ripping out one man's biceps and another man's throat. The gonzo biker crashed head on into the side of what had been a Chevy Family-Mover, catapulting off his bike to lodge half in the side window, the glass ripping his eyes away—

And then Traveler was upon them.

He bisected a chain of screaming metal, ramming the Meat Wagon—his sardonic name for the van—between a triwheeled hawg and an old Apache chopper, his speed built up for a hundred yards to 110 miles per hour till his momentum was enough to kick them easily out of the way: the triwheel, caught on his right front bumper, went spinning like a badly designed Frisbee off to the right, turning end over end till it smashed onto its rider. The chopper crashed into the Meat Wagon's reinforced left rear fender and rebounded. Traveler saw the chopper, wheels over saddle, flying one way, the driver, boots over scarfed head, flying the other. Just up ahead three bikers had regrouped to meet Traveler's attack. They'd broken from the circle and were coming hard at him,

11

two to the left, one to the right. The one on the right had a sawed-off shotgun braced against his right thigh, and with his free hand he was leveling it at Traveler's vulnerable tires. The tires were protected in a half-assed way by swinging swatches of chain link. But that might not be enough. The gunman had priority.

Traveler swung the van to home in on him and reached for the Fire button on the steering column.

The biker was sixty feet off, fifty, and closing. Traveler knew the exact spot in front of the van that would be the cross-hairs point for the HKs.

Fifty feet, forty-five, forty—

He thumb-punched the button, squeezing off two quick bursts of intersecting steel-jacketed death. The snarling biker, his eyes hidden in opaque goggles, hair tied back in a black-scarf headband, threw his arms out as if for crucifixion as the bullets lifted him out of the saddle, lifting him and ripping him both, splitting his gut up the middle so that his insides made blue-red abstracts on the boulder behind him.

Traveler noted all this only with his peripheral vision, already having turned his attention to the two bikers closing on his left. The nearest rode a fire-red chopped Harley, his face almost as red as his bike and his teeth coated with dust—something in his hand . . .

"Shit!" Traveler snarled.

The grenade bounced from the Meat Wagon's armored snout and rolled beneath the van. . . .

Desperately, Traveler stepped on the accelerator, flooring it, hoping that in the one or two seconds left he might be able to get ahead of the blast.

The Meat Wagon seemed to kick up its rear tires like a bucking horse, the blast lifting it half off the ground, and when it came down, it was with a grinding metal sound Traveler hated to hear. He'd lost one or both of the rear tires, and maybe the damned axle as well.

The Meat Wagon fishtailed as he brought it around to face the bikers and the triangle of station wagons.

It jolted to a stop, and there were a few seconds of silence as the dust cleared.

Then, as he reached for the weapons racked behind the front seat, he saw them looming up out of the cloud of yellow. Half a dozen of them. "Come and get it," he murmured, climbing into the rear. He figured them for some variation on roadrats, the footloose bands of scavengers and psychos driven mad with hunger and horror at the end of civilization, the third world war that had ravaged the planet fifteen years before; they were one-time human beings become animals whose favorite occupation, after raping, pillaging, and burning, was simple slaughter. One look in their faces and you knew. . . .

But at the same time he thought: *Where did he get that grenade?*

That kind of armament was hard to come by these days—as was anything that wasn't handmade. Maybe this variation of psycho had some special connections.

No time for further speculations—they were closing in.

He slid open the gunnery slit he'd cut above the left rear fender, stuck the muzzle of the HK91 heavy rifle through, thumbed off the safety, and started squeezing off rounds. He hadn't had to sight in—his target had come to him.

A fat one, a jack-o'-lantern grin on his jowly face, was roaring up to toss another grenade. Traveler squeezed off a short burst of 7.62 NATO cartridges. A less experienced fighter might have made it a long, wasteful burst out of sheer adrenaline-rushed panic or anger. Traveler couldn't afford to waste ammo. And he was as experienced as they come. Back before the war, sixteen years before, in his early twenties, he'd been one of the best— an American commando. Force Recon, the long-range recon patrols, all the gonzo outfits with a rep for being crazy enough to take on *any* mission. And the man Traveler had taken on more than his share. That was before he'd foresworn the name that went with his past life, the name that made him remember the wife and child fried alive in the H-bomb blast that took out New York. . . . That was before he'd become the aimlessly wandering vagabond, the killing machine, the living legend in this postholocaust hell who called himself Traveler.

. . . And the jack-o'-lantern face of the fat biker exploded in a fireworks of red; the grenade had been over the man's right shoulder as he'd prepared to fling it. It fell back with him and exploded with an ear-shivering *whump* that took out a second bike and its shrieking rider.

The other bikes roared by, firing one-handed. Bullets careened off the Meat Wagon's shatterproof front windshield and dented the metal of the doors. Traveler wondered again: *Where are they getting these weapons?*

He heard a shriek behind him and turned.

A big, Levi's-jacketed man, dirty as a month-dead roadside carcass, sagged just inside the left front door of the van. He had opened the door, and the spring-and-tension booby trap which Traveler had installed against

14

intruders had shot four-inch nails into his eyes, carving up his brain.

But there was only one booby trap on that door, and the second biker climbing over his dead buddy seemed to sense that; he laughed, showing yellow teeth and firing a forty-five—no different from Traveler's—point-blank at the place where Traveler had been.

Had been?

The biker looked puzzled—and then his puzzlement cleared up as Traveler launched himself at him from the other corner of the van's rear bed, knife in hand.

The biker had simply never seen anyone move that fast before.

Traveler's combat knife had a seven-inch blade with a black aluminum handle; Traveler had killed with it so many times it was like an extension of him.

He whipped his arm down and drove the blade effortlessly into the biker's throat before the man could recover his composure. The blade made everything the biker drank with, breathed with, and talked with instantly nonfunctional—a shredding of gushing tubes. The man dropped the gun and clawed at the wound, falling back over his dead companion. Traveler recovered from his spring and rolled to the left, sideways, over the refrigeration unit and the spare gas tank, onto the cot, where he jerked the assault rifle free of the slot and whipped it around to face the front door—

No one.

He disengaged the rear door's booby trap and shoved the door open, throwing himself to the ground outside, rolling, coming up with rifle ready in his hand.

No one here either.

Dust. The sun glaring down from almost directly

overhead, making a sinister red-gold halo in the cloud of dust. He squinted against the grit and listened. He could hear the bikes—moving away. But he could see someone's silhouette in the dust, coming toward him.

He raised the gun and waited.

The cloud of yellow . . .

For a split second, time telescoped and bent over backwards for Traveler. He was in another cloud of yellow. Yellow gas: neurotoxins sprayed from the chopper whipping the air not far over the clearing. He was back in El Hiagura, Central America. 1988. He, Orwell, Margolin, and Hill had been out on a routine recon—or so they thought—when the copter from the El Hiaguran army had shuddered up from the trees. What was it Captain Vallone had said? "The area is safe. No sign of government troops." They were supposed to go in to find and support the pro-American guerrillas who were fighting to overthrow the Soviet-backed El Hiaguran government. And Vallone had said there would be no trouble in that sector from government troops. That misinformation had led them to cross that clearing when they should have stayed under cover of the jungle. And the bastards had tested their new Soviet-made weapon on them: neurotoxins. They increased your awareness of things around you till you went mad, your nervous system overloaded. Every scratch from a blade of grass was like the slash of a serrated sword. All four men had gone over the edge. . . . And he'd wakened in a state-side hospital, temporarily restored by an experimental antitoxin serum. A serum the other men hadn't had—they were scattered in other vet hospitals, he'd learned, and waiting for their chance to try the serum. And that was when the Big One hit.

World War III. Lieutenant Kiel Paxton, the man who would one day become Traveler, salvaged a large supply of the neurotoxin serum—which he now kept in the small refrigeration unit in the back of his van, against the day he might find Margolin, Hill, and Orwell. They suffered from the same nerve degeneration—only they didn't have the serum that retarded its effects. One day he'd get it to them. And he'd be reunited with his only buddies. If he could find them. If—

If he lived.

The silhouette in the yellow dust—in the here and now—became a man pointing a rifle at him.

Traveler jerked the assault rifle up to firing position.

But the man said, "For God's sake don't shoot. Not you, too. . . ."

Traveler realized the stranger must be from the station wagon caravan. He stood up and lowered the gun.

The man coughed, as the dust settled around them.

"I want to thank you—" the man began.

"Forget it," Traveler snapped. He scanned the horizon and saw no sign of the bikers.

"Between you and us, we scared 'em off," the stranger said. He was a portly, balding man, his face a mask of sweat-stuck yellow dust, his eyes red-rimmed brown. He was carrying a 30.06 deer rifle.

"Not for long," Traveler said. "I think they're regrouping. Maybe with reinforcements. Something weirdly military about them. The weapons. The attack style. Crazy but—organized." He shrugged and kicked at his rear tires. Both blown out by the grenade. He had two spares up top of the van and a jack. "Give me a hand," he growled. Two other men trotted up and helped them change the tires. They got the last lug in place—and then Traveler felt the bikers approaching.

They were coming back for more, and this time they'd brought help.

Traveler couldn't see them—and he could only barely hear them. But the neurotoxins had unforeseen side effects. They gave him preternaturally keen senses. And another sense, perhaps a sixth sense. Proximity sense, some called it. An animal's ability to sense danger; the primitive raw stuff of intuition. Something long buried in the cerebral cortex and awake only in a few people. Sometimes it gave Traveler an edge.

"Look," the balding man said, licking dust from his lips. "I—we—we need your help. Just a little more. They shot our horses. There's only six of us left. We could just fit in the back of your van here—"

"Forget it," Traveler said flatly. "Take to the desert and hide. I'm not a bus driver."

"We can pay you!" the man shouted as his companions hobbled up. One of them was a pretty girl in her late teens, blue-eyed and blond, an apparition—like a vision of heaven shown to men in hell just to tantalize them.

Traveler tore his eyes from her. "What can you pay me?"

The bikes rumbled louder, getting near.

"Ammo! We've got a crate of 7.62-mm for that assault rifle of yours and maybe those machine guns!" the man shouted. "And more when you get us where we're going."

Traveler sighed. "All right. Get in."

18

2

Between Fists of Steel

The highway stretched empty and almost featureless ahead of them. Behind them—only a few hundred yards away, and gradually closing—the small army of bikers was riding in heavy-metal formation.

Traveler's dead-blue eyes were narrowed; his short sandy hair stuck to his skull with sweat; his hands showed white knuckles on the steering wheel. It wasn't the bikers that had given him the sweats. He was used to human scum of all kinds. It was his new "allies." The six people crammed into the back of the small, stream-lined van made him feel claustrophobic. That was another nasty side effect of the neurotoxins. He could feel each life force individually; he could feel the pressure of six personalities, crammed in where two usually felt like too many.

A loner? Sure, he was a loner. But he hadn't always been. The neurotoxins had made him that way—and the Games. All the games he'd played with Death, always managing to keep just one step ahead of it. Had he stopped to help this bunch because of some linger-ing human feeling? Or because it was another challenge, something to take away the boredom, the nagging emptiness. . . .

Maybe a little of both.

"You said east," Traveler said to Thorne, the balding man who'd spoken for the others. Thorne was riding shotgun.

"Yeah. east. Due east. Thirty miles. Then we cut north a little."

"Where's that take you?" Traveler's voice was cold, disinterested.

"Kansas City," Thorne said.

Traveler looked at him with a flicker of surprise. "Kansas City's still standing?"

Thorne nodded. He kept looking in the rearview mirror and swallowing. "Uh, yeah. Still there. The only major city spared—except mine."

"Yours?"

"Wichita. I'm the foreign minister of Wichita, the Kingdom of Wichita. The king of Wichita sent us on this trip." He shook his head. "We were underprotected. See, when we started out we had three big trucks. Forty men. Lots of protection. And then we hit Drift. You been to Drift?"

Traveler nodded.

"When we got to Drift, we were halfway to Kansas City. Figured to swap for some fuel. . . ."

Traveler could guess what had happened.

Drift was a conglomeration of squatters' huts, Quonsets, shanties, barracks become bordellos, all crowded in without any sense of organization on a deserted military base. Some of the people there sold things; some came to buy—more came to thieve, to cheat, to whore. There was not much authority in Drift, except

20

what each individual "dealership" provided in the form of surly bouncers. Bouncers? *Crushers* would be a better word. Almost anything could be bought in Drift; in the postholocaust world *everything* was black market. No other market existed, unless you dealt with the president out in Vegas and his fanatic soldiers, the Glory Boys. And if you got too close to the Glory Boys—what was left of the U.S. military—you might find yourself "drafted." Which meant enslaved.

"Don't tell me," Traveler said. "You were dumb enough to leave the trucks without a guard. . . ."

"We had guards!" Thorne retorted defensively.

"How many?"

"Well . . ." Thorne looked sheepish. "Only two stayed with the trucks. The others went into the tavern. We'd been traveling a long time. Had some close calls. We came back out when we heard the guards screaming and the trucks start up. But it was too late. Whoever it was stabbed the guards, took the trucks, and drove off with them. I had to trade nearly all our jewelry for the wagons and supplies. I couldn't go back to Wichita after losing . . ." He let it trail off.

Traveler gave an almost imperceptible nod. "You fucked up, so you couldn't go back. They wouldn't have bought this bullshit about being 'underprotected.' "

Someone in the back laughed, hearing that.

"What happened after Drift?" Traveler asked. He could feel the presence of the girl in the back strongly. He had to force himself to keep from turning around. It had been a long time. . . .

And he could feel her looking at him.

"After Drift we hired six wagons. The drivers turned out to be crooks. Killed nearly half my men in their sleep, ran off with half our stuff. Three wagons left. Roadrats hit us, killed maybe ten, twelve more. That was yesterday. We were lucky to get away with our lives. God help the poor bastards we had to leave behind."

Traveler knew what he meant. The roadrats had one favorite sport: torture.

As he drove he glanced at the Geiger counter he'd bolted to the dash. They hadn't hit a hot spot yet. He knew the southwest; he knew the crumbling new coastline of California; he knew the Shocklands of Texas—but he hadn't drifted this far north in his fifteen years as mercenary vagabond. And the information about the distribution of radiation hot spots was rarely accurate.

Thorne was silent for a while. Finally, Traveler said, "Well? I'm waiting."

"Huh?"

"Why the hell did you go on this stupid suicide trip anyway?"

"Oh." Thorne cleared his throat and looked doubtfully over his shoulder at the others.

There was the girl, Sandy. Late teens or early twenties. Looking young but acting older, more cynical than she ought to be. Hell, she was lucky not to be completely psycho—World War III had twisted most of the children who'd survived, had taken away their hope for a future, their will to live. She'd grown up in Wichita—but even if the city had been spared, it had to be like the few others that hadn't been hit: an armed camp, surrounded by wasteland and enemies; a slum and a hotbed for disease and pestilence. Not a joyous place to grow up in.

There was the tall, goony one, Pratt. Pratt was always prattling, trying to laugh it up, a believer in joking your troubles away. A pain in the ass. He wore thick glasses, and his Adam's apple was always bobbing on his long neck.

There was Mortner, a sad-eyed bulldog of a man always predicting doom; he laughed only in contempt, or at morbid humor.

There was a fresh-faced blond kid, Scott, maybe nineteen. One of the surviving guards. He kept trying not to look at Sandy.

In the back, leaning against the door, rifle across his knees, was Pearlman, a bull of a man with thick eyebrows. He smiled at nothing. He was a pro, like Traveler.

Mortner looked sorrowfully up at Thorne and smiled the smile of the defeated. "Are you kidding, Thorne? Tell him! He's all we've got!"

Thorne looked at Sandy. She nodded. "Tell him. If he's going to take us where we're going—"

"No," Traveler said abruptly. "Not into that town. I don't go into towns. Just as far as the nearest squat-shelter where you can hire something else."

Thorne cleared his throat. "We haven't got the money to hire anything more. We're out of jewelry. We've got that ammo—and there'll be a fat reward for you in Kansas City."

Traveler sighed. Fat reward? Money meant nothing anymore. A few places still took U.S. dollars because you could trade them to the Vegas Glory Boys for supplies—or you could have, once. He'd heard recently they'd stopped taking them. The commodity now, when you were dealing with the remnants of the U.S.

government, was human flesh. Your children, your prisoners—for "special training." Or special "experiments" conducted by the government's secret underground labs. . . . But come the rise and fall of every civilization, gold and jewels had always been valuable. Along with fuel and food—mostly canned goods, scarcer each year— weapons, ammo, and gold were the basic currency.

"You still didn't tell me . . ." Traveler said. He glanced in his side door mirror. The bikers were gaining on him.

Thorne cleared his throat again. "It's like this: The king of Wichita and the baron of Kansas City have made a pact. By radio, you see. We are to unite our two kingdoms—"

"What is this *medieval* bullshit?" Traveler asked, amazed.

Thorne seemed offended. "The baron decided that what with the breakdown of civilization, his people needed order—of the simplest and most basic kind. So he and his, uh—"

"His army of thugs," Traveler prompted.

"Ha! He's right about *that*!" Mortner cawed. Traveler winced.

"Yes, well," Thorne was saying, "the baron and his *army* established a sort of feudal arrangement. He tried to take over Wichita too—we beat him and his men back. Our people captured some of theirs, and when the king—he wasn't a king then, he was calling himself mayor—when he heard from the prisoners about the old-fashioned feudal set-up in Kansas City, he decided, uh . . ."

"Decided he'd like to be a megalomaniac too," Traveler suggested.

Sandy laughed.

Pratt pretended to.

Thorne shrugged. "Anyway—we kept coming into conflict with Kansas City. So—it was decided to merge the two cities. Or kingdoms. The old-fashioned way—by blood. Sandy here is the daughter of our king. She's going to marry the baron's son."

Traveler looked at him. "Are you serious? You're not putting me on? You risked this girl's life for a fairy tale?"

Thorne blew out his cheeks. "We had to start somewhere. The people needed something . . . something romantic . . ."

Traveler shook his head in disbelief. "Jesus Christ."

"We're most of the way there," Sandy said suddenly. "Can't you take us the rest of the way?"

Traveler said, "I'll think about it. That off-road you're taking—what kind of road is it?"

"Partly concrete, partly gravel and dirt. The main road to the city was washed out in the Aftermath Floods," Thorne said, squinting at his map.

"It'll be slower going there," Traveler said, swerving to avoid an overturned car and an intermingled heap of skeletons. "We'll be sitting ducks for the bikers."

"It'll be slower going for them too," Sandy pointed out. "Maybe harder for them."

Traveler nodded. He had to admit she was right. She was a strong, intelligent girl.

Traveler checked his gas gauge. "How long down that side road?"

Thorne glanced at the map. "About seventy miles."

Traveler sighed. "Don't think I have enough fuel."

"What are you burning?" Sandy asked. "Smells . . . funny."

"Maybe it's *laughing gas*, then!" Pratt said brightly. No one laughed.

"Tequila," Traveler told her. "Seven-gallon jugs of it. Traded some . . . work for it. This engine will run on anything that burns. Perfume, alcohol, gasoline, booze. Anything."

"Not enough fuel," Mortner was saying. "I knew it. That's it. We're dead, then."

"Shut up," said Pearlman. It was the first time he'd spoken. "You the one they call Traveler?" Pearlman asked.

Without turning around, Traveler nodded.

"Listen, Traveler," Pearlman growled. "We can get fuel. We can take it. I'll help. You and me. We'll team it."

Traveler nodded. They'd have to steal the fuel from roadrats. He had a feeling that Pearlman was capable of the necessary mayhem.

"You'll do it?" Mortner said, surprised.

Traveler said, "I'll get you there—for all the supplies I can carry out with me. Of my choosing. And a pound of gold."

Thorne winced. "Okay—I'll arrange it."

Traveler looked in the side mirror. The bikers—had vanished.

He frowned.

"Looks like this is the turnoff," Thorne said.

"Looks like it's turn or die," Sandy remarked.

Up ahead the highway ended in a fissure. The far side of the fissure was at least twenty yards away. No telling how deep it was. It was one of the big cracks that had opened up in the earth's crust after World War III.

A narrower stretch of broken concrete road curved off to the right. Traveler swung onto it and accelerated. He had an idea what had happened to the bikers—they'd gone across country to cut him off. He shouted at Pearlman. "Can you use that HK91 in the gun rack?"

Pearlman nodded and put aside the smaller rifle. Scott took it; Pearlman picked up the heavy assault rifle and pushed open the firing slit above the left rear wheel, poking the muzzle through. "Thorne, get in back," Traveler barked.

Thorne, looking nervously out the window, was only too glad to comply. He'd seen the same thing Traveler had.

There was a big, nasty mess of roadrats up ahead.

3

Rats Will Eat Anything, They Say

Roadrats ahead. Bikers to one side. And lots of both.

Traveler had a feeling someone had set Thorne's little peacemaking mission up for failure. Failure because the mission would never show up. Who was it, Traveler wondered, who had equipped the bikers with the grenades? And who had tipped off the roadrats?

The roadrats were a hundred yards ahead, their vehicles behind a barricade blocking the road. Maybe thirty rats in all. A big band, or two bands combined. Some of them were fanning out to either side of the road in cars or on horseback.

Traveler had reloaded the machine guns, but that wouldn't get them through the barrier.

How the hell, he asked himself, did you get into this one?

More to the point, how are you going to get out of it?

Go around it? But the ambushers had picked the spot carefully: the wastelands to both sides were boulder-strewn, choked with the foundations of the shopping center that had once stood there; impassable. He'd have to go through the barrier, or back.

The barrier loomed up ahead.

Scott climbed into the passenger seat, the deer rifle in his hands, looking to Traveler nervously.

Traveler looked out the side window and saw the wastelands alive with chrome and black leather. The Horde. The bikers.

The barrier was sixty yards ahead.

Traveler smiled. He stopped the Meat Wagon in the middle of the road; it was canted forty-five degrees from the road's centerline. He climbed over Scott and opened the side door, got out on the right. The angle of the van partly protected him from roadrat sniper fire.

They could see him, though, and they stared in amazement. No one had expected this move. He hoped their surprise and curiosity would keep them off-balance just long enough. . . .

He had seen the outrider from the Horde and hoped these geeks operated in the traditional tribal style.

The choppers came weaving in and out of obstructions but roughly keeping to a V-formation; the desolate plains shivered with the waves of roaring sound as the bikes came on. Riding out front of the V-point was a shaggy bear of a man wearing an old leather flight jacket and blacked goggles. The frame of his bike bristled with spikes.

Traveler raised his arm over his head and slowly lowered it, so it pointed straight out in front of him, the hand fisted—pointing at the outrider.

It was a hand-sign recognized by most roadrats and wasteland vagabonds. It meant: *I challenge you*.

Then he held up both arms to show he was carrying no guns. He wore only his knife.

The outrider grinned and pulled up short sixty feet

29

away. He signaled to the rest of the band, and they pulled up behind him, wakes of dust continuing on in the slight breeze made by their movement to momentarily engulf them.

The outrider got off his massive bike and killed the engine. He made a sign, the old Italian sign for Up Yours. That meant he accepted the challenge.

It was only a temporary reprieve. Traveler knew that. Even if he defeated this man, the Horde and the roadrats would come down on him. But it gave him time to work out the scheme that had come to mind.

"Scott," he said over his shoulder. "Can you drive that van?"

"Sure!"

"Okay. There's two things I want you to do. There's a package in brown wax paper in the weapons compartment. Take it and put it under your shirt. When I'm busy with this guy, stay as close as you can to me without making it look like you're going to help. When I give you the signal, toss me the package, then get into the van and follow me."

"Follow you?"

"You'll see. Do it. And leave the rifle behind."

"Uh—okay."

The outrider was approaching, on foot, grinning, a meat cleaver in his right hand.

Traveler walked toward him, fast, hoping to keep the fight within the vicinity of the bike. It was a three-wheel monster, stripped to give maximum room to its oversized engine. It gleamed like a chrome giant insect in the hot afternoon sun.

The two men came to within two yards of each other,

twenty feet from the bike. Scott—weaponless—squatted about thirty feet off to Traveler's right.

"What's with the kid?" the bearish man asked, frowning. It was difficult to see his frown, since most of his face was a shag of black beard. And his eyes were hidden in goggles. The expression showed only in his wrinkled forehead, where layers of dust and grime creased.

"I'm teaching him something," Traveler said. "He wanted to learn how to kill, so I'm going to show him. He's just going to watch. That's all."

The biker laughed, and Traveler could smell the laugh. It smelled like a rabbit left dead by the road for two weeks.

"You're a pretty confident little shit," the biker said. "That's good. I get fun from busting up guys who think they're king of the hill."

"You gonna talk all day?" Traveler asked.

The grime creased again. The big man tore off his goggles and flung them aside. The skin was skull-colored under the goggles, marked out by rings of yellow dust. His eyes were so red the original color couldn't be made out. They flared like windows into a furnace. The guy was about six three, at least 220 pounds.

Traveler was only about five nine; he was not bulge-muscled like his opponent. But, looking Traveler over, the big man knew better than to underestimate the smaller man. Traveler just stood there, loose-limbed, calm. No visible trace of tension. He was muscled like a panther and moved with a panther's grace.

Concealed in his belt, Traveler had three ninja shuriken, the four-pointed hardened-steel killing stars used by martial arts experts. The ninja stars were only

31

three and a half inches in diameter. And yet, hurled by a skilled hand, they could be deadly. But one of the things that sustained Traveler's sanity in the hell the world had become was his sense of sportsmanship. When possible, he fought fair.

It wasn't always possible. And sometimes a man had to make an art of doing dirty to his opponent.

The big man lumbered toward him, raising the cleaver. The razor-sharp edge of the blade was licked by a flash of afternoon sun. The sun was to their right.

Traveler maneuvered for the oldest trick in the world: He circled so the sun would be in his opponent's eyes.

The big man blinked and rushed in.

Traveler had drawn the knife from its sheath. He leaped effortlessly to one side, slashing. The cleaver came grinding down on the granite face of a boulder, shooting blue sparks. Traveler's slash made a small cut in the big man's dusty leather jacket. That was all. He danced back. He was faster, but the other man had a longer reach. He maneuvered the fight toward the motorcycle, his back to it now, ducking whistling swipes of the cleaver, striking with his knife. He managed to slash the back of the big man's hand so blood spurted onto the cleaver and dripped down to be sucked up by the thirsty sands. But the cut only made the big man madder.

He charged Traveler, moving faster than should have been possible for one of his bulk, and enclosed Traveler's left wrist in his stubby vise-strong fingers, squeezing so hard the wrist-bones squeaked, threatened to break.

Traveler's face showed no emotion; he was used to ignoring pain.

The cleaver was whistling straight down from overhead,

32

aimed for his forehead. It would cleave him between the eyes and split his brain into its two halves neatly as a walnut coming apart under a kitchen knife.

Traveler snapped his head to the right, so hard and fast the bones in his neck creaked, then whipped it back in the same second, cracking it sideways into the flat of the cleaver blade, all the force in his neck and shoulder muscles deflecting the cleaver so it missed his neck and sank into the aging Kevlar shoulder pads of his flak jacket.

The synthetic slowed the blade; by the time it had cut through and reached the flesh beneath, most of its force was spent. It dug only a fraction of an inch into the flesh of his left shoulder. But . . .

It hurt like hell.

The pain gushed adrenaline through him, and he pulled the biker off his feet, back on top of him—and over, in a judo roll, so the big man lost his hold on Traveler and flipped onto his back, grunting, the breath knocked out of him. For a split second the two men lay head to head, legs pointed away from a mutual center like the two hands on the clock of mortality. And then Traveler was up, turning, grabbing the man's beard and using it to jerk the snarling head back so he could get at the throat. With snake-striking speed Traveler slashed out the man's throat. Then, for good measure, he drove the knife through the leather jacket and into the biker's heart. He didn't know it, but he'd stuck the blade right through a tattoo that said *Born To Die Young* against a blue heart-shape.

Traveler dragged the knife from the biker, sheathed it, and shouted, "Scott!" as he heard the bikes start up again. The Horde was coming.

Scott tosssed him the brown paper package. Traveler caught it like a forward pass and sprinted to the big bike. The keys were in the ignition.

As Scott ran for the van, and as the bikers roared nearer from the other side, Traveler tore open a corner of the package and plunged a small clockwork detonator into the plastic mass. *One minute ten seconds*. He stuck the package in the bike's saddlebag and started the engine, snapping it into gear. He grabbed the handlebars and twisted the throttle. The bike roared up like a wild thing with a life of its own, its front end lifting clear of the ground as the big rear wheels spun. And then it rocketed across the plain toward the roadrat barrier. The bikers were nearly on top of him. A big one just four feet to the right was spinning a chain overhead like a lasso. He lashed it across Traveler's right arm, which promptly went numb. Traveler accelerated, temporarily out of reach.

"Shit," Traveler grunted through the spray of grit flying into his face from the churning wheels. A cloud of dust had enveloped them. He had a glimpse of the flanking roadrats coming in from their outside positions to trap him and the van between. He was completely surrounded by bikers and roadrats. His right arm wasn't much use; he had to control the rollicking handlebars with his left, barely managed to hold on, and was several times nearly bounced from the saddle as he struck potholes and small boulders in the wasteland. The barrier loomed up ahead.

He could see the silhouettes of the roadrats through the dust, their guns converging on him. He drove at what he thought was the weak link in their chain, a place where two smaller cars were parked nose to nose

34

behind a barrier of scrap wood and swatches of hurricane fence.

He slowed, mentally counting off the seconds. . . .

He was nearly atop the barrier. He jumped onto the saddle, then leapt from it to the biker who'd hit him with the chain, using the heavy man's body to cushion his impact as they were both carried gasping onto the dirt, thirty feet short of the barrier.

There was a long, distended moment of flash-pains and the world rocking, spinning. Then he found himself lying beside the man he'd knocked off the bike. The man's head lolled at an odd angle. His neck was broken.

The bike with the bomb in it struck the barrier and plowed into it, bending it back, enclosing itself in strands of metal and slats of wood. Traveler stared. Why didn't it—

The explosion made him duck his head. He glimpsed a fireball growing like a flower blooming in fast-action cinema. Bits and pieces of men, fences, and cars flying helter-skelter. Several bikes lay on their sides, men getting muzzily to their knees, knocked over by the force of the blast.

The van pulled up beside Traveler, its right side door swinging open. Traveler forced himself up, and in.

Scott floored it, and the Meat Wagon leapt through the gap made by the explosion, between the two cars flung onto their backs like overturned turtles, bouncing on its shocks as it ground relentlessly over the dead and dying.

Traveler reached in back, jerked his shotgun free of its sling, and swung it to the still-open, swinging side door, firing at the blurred roadrat faces as the human scum tried to stop the van from getting through. The shotgun blasted and the faces screamed, fell away disfigured. The Meat Wagon lurched on, and out of the dust cloud. Pearlman used the automatic rifle to discourage the bikers who tried to follow them, cutting down half a dozen.

The highway stretched clear and empty before them.

4

Trading Death for Perfume

They had a considerable lead on both the roadrats and the bikers. But it couldn't last, Traveler knew. He'd have to lose them.

Up ahead the road diverged around the prow of a wedge-shaped hill. To the right was a dirt road that very soon turned a corner. To the left the cracked asphalt continued on. "To the left!" Thorne shouted, looking at the map. But Traveler cut to the right.

"What the hell are you—"

"Shut up," Traveler snapped. He drove hard down the dirt road to the first curve, deliberately fishtailing to raise more dust. When he reached the curve, he stopped and backed up, staying roughly in his own tracks. He backed to the asphalt, then took the left-hand road, following the asphalt around the curve.

Two minutes later a small army of bikers and roadrats arrived and approached the fork in the road. They slowed, and then the man in the lead pointed to the dirt road—where Traveler's dust was still hanging in the air, slowly settling.

The bikers led the roadrats onto the dirt track, the wrong way. The Horde thundered into the wastelands.

Traveler drove on, following the highway, gunning the engine to its fullest—nearly 110 miles per hour.

It would go 140 without so much human baggage.

He checked the fuel gauge. Nearly empty. And his auxiliary tank was empty. It was late afternoon. Twilight soon.

They'd have to find another source of fuel, and quick.

Twenty minutes later he spotted a thin spiral of smoke that hinted of a settlement or a camp up ahead. He pulled off the road, into a hollow between three snugged hills, and concealed the van in the ruins of an old prewar structure, now weathered and burnt past recognition. A thousand or more travelers had stopped over here since the war; the cement floor was blackened with campfire char, the walls smothered in graffiti.

They camouflaged the van in the shadowy back of the roofless structure, covering it with old sheets of plywood and wallpaper.

"But—what are we doing here?" Mortner whined. "There's hours of daylight left. We could—"

"Out of fuel," Traveler said shortly.

"Out of fuel! What are we gonna do?" He sat on a dusty wooden box and stared dejectedly at the graffiti on the wall. "They'll kill us," he whispered to himself. "But then I should have expected it."

"Oh, come on, Bill!" Pratt chimed in. "We'll be cozy as a bug in a rug here!"

Traveler looked at Pratt, then controlled his temper. If he gagged Pratt, as he had just considered doing, Mortner would get more frightened, and he'd have to gag him too. Too much trouble.

Sandy helped them camouflage the van, then asked, "Should we build a fire?"

Traveler shook his head. "Smoke might attract attention. I'm just *hoping* we lost those scumbags back there—but they might get wise and retrace their steps." He and Sandy stood close together. He was surprised to smell perfume. Jasmine, if he remembered right. But then, she was one of the elite in the Kingdom of Wichita. She probably had one of the few bottles remaining. . . .

For a moment he closed his eyes and breathed it and remembered women. Women as they used to be.

"Why is it you never look at me?" Sandy asked softly, interrupting the ugly memory. "You look at the others when you talk to them."

"Stupid question," Traveler said and walked away.

But he *had* been looking at her. Covertly. She wore faded jeans, clean white tennis shoes (where had she got those? They looked new) a dust-streaked white blouse. Her breasts, pointed and well separated, strained at the fabric. Her ass was firm and round; her face was clear-skinned, her eyes unsullied by horror. Her long, healthy-looking blond hair was tied back in a ponytail. He wasn't used to seeing people look so clean, well fed, and healthy. There were probably only a few hundred like that left on the continent.

He found himself wondering when he'd last taken a bath.

"Forget it," he muttered to himself and went to post the guards. He put Scott and Mortner together at one broken-down door; Thorne at the other. He gave Scott the light assault rifle.

"What about me?" Sandy asked. "I can shoot."

39

He gave her the deer rifle and forced himself to look at her as he did.

She smiled, and involuntarily, he smiled back.

Suddenly, he felt like a fool.

"Uh . . ." he said, looking around. "There. The window. You cover the window." He turned with an excess of businesslike briskness to Pearlman. "You reload that thing?"

Pearlman nodded.

"We set out soon as it gets toward sunset," Traveler said. "I want to see the place in the light before I hit it in the dark."

Sandy said, "Why did we camouflage the van if we're all going to be out here in plain sight?"

Traveler shrugged. "They might come while I'm gone. They might kill you and your friends. They might miss the van—and I'd be pleased if they missed the van. They get real caught up in torturing sometimes, so they just might not spot it right away."

She stared at him, white-faced, and turned away. "Oh."

He turned to Pearlman and said, "If you can, get up on that piece of roof that's left. I'll see some food's brought to you, if there is any."

Pearlman grunted and went to his post, climbing the rubble to get there.

For a moment Traveler stared abstractedly at the graffiti. His nerves had been sizzled in that hit on the roadrats. He could hear Mortner's breathing. And Scott's breathing. And Sandy's and Pratt's. He could hear a small animal, probably a lizard judging by the rasp of its dragged tail, scuttling through the rubble. He could feel every thread in his fatigues. He needed something.

40

A drink would have to do. The graffiti seemed to leap out at him:

THE SOUTHERN WARRIORS ARE GOING TO EAT YOU ALIVE and SUCK MY TARANTULA and WELCOME TO MY NIGHTMARE and WHEN THE HOTRIDERS GET YOU THEY'LL MAKE YOU PAY FOR BEING BORN and the usual selection of obscenities.

He slipped between the slats of plywood and edged up to the side door of the narrow space containing the van, squeezed himself in, and froze.

Sandy was in the back, bending over a crate of their supplies. He could see well into her cleavage, and it looked like the gates of heaven.

He forced himself to look away and cleared his throat.

She looked up, and smiled, blushing. She sat up straight.

"You hungry?" she asked.

"Yeah."

She gave him four tin cans and a can opener. "Pass 'em out, okay?" she asked. "I'll bring out some other stuff."

He turned to the refrigeration unit, opened it, and took out a jar of clear fluid. He opened it, took a healthy swallow, grimaced, and replaced it in the unit.

"What was that?" she asked. And then, hopefully, "Drugs?"

He had to smile. "No, the last of the tequila. I didn't put it all in the tank. I had some nerve damage, and it calms the nerves."

Already he could feel the coolness washing through him, the receding of the painful sensory input.

His arms filled with tin cans, he backed out of the van.

He passed out the food, then looked at the can he'd kept for himself. He swore, and tossed it to Mortner.

It was pork and beans.

Traveler and Pearlman were lying on their bellies atop a small hill overlooking the roadrat encampment.

"You think that's it?" Pearlman said, pointing.

He indicated a tent whose doorflap was half open. Through the flap they could just make out a number of army surplus gas cans.

"Probably."

"How we going to get it back to our camp, supposing we get to it alive?"

Traveler hooked a thumb at the big plastic "bladder" he'd brought along. "Inflatable. Carries about fifteen gallons of anything. We carry that to the roadrat camp. As for how we're going to get it out—I dunno. Got any bright ideas?"

Pearlman frowned. "Going to be heavy and awkward. Some kind of cart's the only way. Or—we could sling it over a horse."

Traveler nodded. "I was just thinking the same thing."

"But that means we'll have to steal a horse," Pearlman observed.

"Yeah. Can you move quietly?"

"I ain't built like Peter Pan, buddy."

"Okay. I'll get the horse. . . ." He studied the layout of the camp.

It was strung out along the floor of a shallow canyon between two ridges. There were about eight tents, most of them made of thick plastic of the sort once used for covering furniture. The tents were translucent, though badly soiled by dust and unidentified muck. They were simple A-shape tents, except a big one in the center that might belong to the chieftain. Traveler could see the foggy outlines of men inside the tents, squatting, moving a little. A few others were outside poking at cooking fires. The vehicles were at either end of the camp, partly blocking entry. There were two horse-drawn station wagons, a couple of pickups, a sort of chariot.

"It's them," Pearlman muttered.

"Who?"

"The bastards who hit us the other day. Took those wagons from us. Killed the others." He didn't sound as if he were deeply aggrieved. Only mildly annoyed. He had been inconvenienced.

"I count maybe . . . ten men."

Pearlman nodded. "That take into account those sentries?"

Traveler grunted in confirmation. There were two sentries at the entrance to the narrow box canyon. It was only about forty feet wide at its widest point, narrowing to twenty feet at the entrance. "There's got to be at least one other—up here somewhere."

Pearlman looked around, raising his head like a dog sniffing the wind.

Traveler said, "Probably over there—see that bunch of boulders on the ridge?" He pointed across the canyon. On a high point of the ridge overlooking the canyon were seven or eight man-sized boulders. The shadows were thickening between them, and Traveler saw one of the shadows move. "See that?" he asked softly.

"I see it," Pearlman whispered. "You think they see us?"

"I doubt it. I figure they're mostly watching the

entrance to the canyon. And every so often they look down at the road to see if anyone's coming. I've got a hypothesis that they're not watching their rear much because it's all wasteland out there. I'm gonna test that hypothesis."

This time Traveler had come well armed.

He had the Colt strapped to his hip, the 12-gauge pump slung on a strap over his shoulder. He left that with Pearlman. He took along the mini-crossbow. It had a light, one-piece stock made out of polypropylene. The 150-pound bow was equipped with a high-power scope. He had three eight-inch arrows. Perfect for the kind of assault he had in mind.

The sun was tipping over the horizon, flinging a last few streamers of red-gold over its shoulder before it went. The shadows were pooling in hollows and darkening under boulders; the ground had taken on a blue-gray cast.

Traveler backed out of their concealed vantage and down the slope. He moved quickly and quietly, stepping carefully so as not to make rocks rattle loose on the hillside. Any noise might alert his victims.

The canyon ended about forty yards to the north of where Pearlman was waiting. The sun was setting behind them; the canyon ran east-west. The sentries were on the eastern rim.

Traveler skirted the edge of the canyon, concealed from the men on the other side by the rimrock rising above him. He reached the end of the fissure and moved in quick bursts from one concealment to the next, merging with the shadows. He reached the far side of the canyon and moved down the hillside so he could come up behind the tumble of boulders.

He climbed up the slope behind them in a zig-zag, freezing once for five minutes after a misstep sent rock tumbling down beneath him. There was no answering motion from above. He continued his ascent.

He reached the tumble of boulders and saw two men on their haunches beside a kerosene lamp, throwing dice.

He smiled.

You both lose, he thought, raising the crossbow. It was cocked and ready. He sighted through the scope on the one who was bent over staring skeptically at the die. The other was looking west, out through a gap in the boulders at the highway across the canyon.

The bow could kill silently. With luck, he could put a bolt through the one looking at the dice and reload before the other realized what was happening.

He fired, and the bolt sang in a beautifully straight line through the dusk. It sank to half its length in the right temple of the man bending over the die. The man sagged forward silently.

His friend glanced at him, then back at the highway—and then did a double take, looking at his compadre more closely.

By this time Traveler had loaded the second bolt.

The sentry stood up to shout a warning. But he couldn't shout because he had an arrow through his larynx. Traveler moved in and finished the man with his knife.

He heard a scrabbling noise behind and spun.

A man with a big gun in his hands was grinning at

45

him. He was a bearded, yellow-haired man whose nose had been hacked away at some point. He was pointing the gun at Traveler's head.

So there was a third sentry, after all.

5

Blood and Darkness Flow Together

"Drop that Robin Hood thing," said the roadrat. His voice had a strange squeak to it due to his lack of a nose.

Traveler hesitated. The guy wanted to take him down to the camp for interrogation—and torture. He had to pretend to go along, for now.

He dropped the crossbow into the dirt. The roadrat watched it fall.

"Now the gunbelt."

Traveler reached down to unbuckle the belt. He did most of the unbuckling with one hand; the other was reaching into the slot cut into the belt leather. He dropped the gunbelt.

Traveler watched the roadrat's face.

The roadrat's piggish eyes followed the belt as it dropped—for that half second the man wasn't watching Traveler's hands.

Traveler plucked out the ninja star and, in the same motion, raised it over his shoulder and flung it from between index finger and thumb. It spun on edge and sank two of its teeth into the biceps of the roadrat's gun arm. The man yelped and reflexively jerked the gun hand up so it was no longer pointed at Traveler.

Traveler lunged, catching the man about the waist, knocking him back in a football tackle. The gun was flung clear.

The man opened his mouth to scream for help.

Traveler jammed his left hand full into the man's mouth and shoved it down his throat. The roadrat made only choking, mewling noises. Hopefully nothing loud enough to hear in the canyon below.

It was disgusting, shoving his fist down this human scum's throat. But it shut him up.

He held the roadrat down, knees on his arms, whipped his knife out, and drove it through one of the man's eyes into his brain.

As the knife came down, there was a flicker-instant in which the roadrat saw his destiny closing in on him, saw the knife coming, knew what it meant. His eyes dilated and he screamed—but the scream was blocked by Traveler's right hand. It stayed in the roadrat's throat. . . . And Traveler could feel that scream vibrating through his flesh and into his bone.

Then the knife bit home and put the thug's lights out for good.

Traveler drew back, cleansing knife and arm, and resting a moment. That scream vibrating through his arm—he could still feel it. It gave him a chill.

He looked at the corpse and wondered: who had this guy been before the war? Maybe a decent guy. Maybe a high school PE teacher. Maybe the owner of a hardware store. Maybe a guy who'd loved his kids. Anyone. And then the hell had been unleashed by the ex-movie-star cowboy-minded president the country had elected hoping for a quick economic fix. And he'd led them into the Dark Ages. So that perfectly decent men were driven mad and became animals. Roadrats.

He shrugged, standing. There was no use brooding about it. They had become animals, and they couldn't be rehumanized. It was too late for the roadrats. So Traveler would have to kill them when they snapped at his legs.

And hope, in the process, he didn't become an animal himself.

He gathered up his arrows, cleaned them off, stuck them in his belt, and worked his way back to Pearlman.

"Trouble?" Pearlman asked.

Traveler nodded. "A little." He wished they'd brought supplies with them. He was feeling hunger and fatigue. "Let's do it."

"How?"

"Play it by ear." With the inflatable fuel bladder looped around Pearlman's shoulders, they trotted down the hillside and circled to approach the roadrats' camp.

Pearlman led the way through a warren of boulders tinged by sunset, puddled beneath by shadow.

The darkness was complete in the entrance to the box canyon. Inky. Gradually, their eyes adjusted a little—but it was too dark for Pearlman to go first. Traveler said, "Let me take the lead. I—got a knack for dark places." Traveler took the lead.

This was another occasion when the neurotoxin curse became a paradoxical blessing. His adrenaline-crisp nerves were fully awake now, the neurotoxin sharpening them to an unnatural pitch of acuity. He could see almost three times more in the darkness than Pearlman could. He could sense the nearness of unseen objects—a boulder looming up, a bat flapping by.

Before the Final War he'd heard of a talent that a great many blind people were said to have, something researchers called "facial vision." The totally blind would walk through an unfamiliar room and suddenly stop before bumping into walls or furniture. They said they could "feel" the wall ahead—in their faces, in the skin itself. Every object has a faint electric charge and slight changes of air pressure and temperature around it. The blind, with their compensatory acuity of the remaining senses, were probably sensing those changes. Traveler's facial vision was unusually well developed. He was nearly as comfortable in the pitch dark as the blind bats swooping just overhead.

Pearlman stumbled along behind him, biting off his curses.

They turned a corner in the angular entrance to the canyon—and froze. Light was flickering up ahead.

"Campfires," Traveler muttered. He could make out the hulking shapes of the roadrats' cars and trucks; one of the shapes moved, a horse shifting in its traces.

They were about fifteen yards away. There were two guards, there. One sitting on the hood of a half-ton pickup, leaning back against the window. Traveler could just make him out. He had a rifle across his lap.

The other was leaning back against the rear of a station wagon. They were talking in low voices. Something about "that scuzzy Drift cunt."

Traveler and Pearlman moved in, creeping along near the rock wall; moving slowly as shadows growing long in a desert afternoon.

At last they were just twelve feet to the right of their

victims. The two guards muttered to one another as the assassins crept closer. A horse snorted uneasily and pricked up its ears.

Both men knew the kill had to be quiet or the raid was useless.

And they knew it had to be done with simultaneous precision; the guards had to be killed at the same moment to prevent them from shouting.

Cold sweat, creeping like a spider, ran down the middle of Traveler's back. He could hear his own heart thudding in his chest.

When they reached the half-ton truck, they split up. Pearlman, crouching, slipped around to the rear. Traveler moved around the front, flowing like something liquid, every muscle as slack as he could make it. The crossbow was in his hands; the shotgun across his back.

Pearlman climbed into the rear of the truck, crept along the truck-bed carefully so as not to make it creak, climbed atop the cab—

Traveler was in position at the grill of the truck. He snapped up to a kneeling pose and fired the crossbow shaft at the standing roadrat. His target had just turned to stare at him, gaping—and the shaft sank to half its length in one of those staring eyes, penetrating the brain. At the same moment Pearlman clapped one big hand over the other one's mouth, and with his knife hand reached under the man's chin and drew the blade through the soft, living flesh, releasing a spurt of blood which looked black as oil in the dimness as it pattered onto the hood between the dying man's knees.

The man spasmed briefly. The horses snorted and champed, but didn't bolt. And then it was over.

Pearlman eased the corpse onto the hood and climbed

down from the truck. The other roadrat corpse simply slid to its knees and stayed there, locked in a position of prayer, praying for mercy from the judges of Hades.

"Get one of those horses loose," Traveler whispered. "Tie it to this bumper here. Then we'll go in."

Pearlman nodded. Making soft noises to comfort the horses, he moved to the traces, unhitched the nearest, and led it to the front of the truck; he did all this slowly so as not to startle the horse or make a suspicious movement that could attract attention from the campfires.

Minute later they were moving into the camp, knives and crossbow ready, each one silently cursing himself for a fool. The odds were, sneaking into the camp—the fuel was kept in the center—they'd be noticed.

Odds were, they were moving with great stealth to their deaths.

6

The Hungry Ones Find Their Meat

He called himself Harley Crater, and he was the chief of the Hungry Ones. They weren't much of a tribe as roadrat tribes go. Only five of them left. They had one car and a chopper. Harley rode the Harley. Ugly Bro drove the old Ford sedan. Merle, his brother Berle, and Ned rode in the battered blue sedan.

Mostly the Hungry Ones lived by scavenging. But they'd gotten themselves a gig riding with the Horde the Glory Boys sent out to stop the peace mission from Wichita.

Only, Harley Crater had got them lost.

They'd been tailing along fine behind the rest of the roadrat horde, behind the bikers, everyone trying to catch up with the bastard who'd broken through the roadblock . . . the guy who'd wasted Fat Ear and Fred, two Hungry Ones, blowing them away with that damned shotgun after he blasted through the blockade.

Crater was almost grateful, secretly; Fat Ear and Fred had both been a pain in the ass. And now he could collect their share of the payoff. If they found the guy.

One guy? Really? That's what the Black Rider had said. "I know that van," the Black Rider had said when Meat Ax had gone out to fight the guy. "That's the one they call Traveler. It's him we got to get. The others are easy."

Crater had thought: *One guy? Bullshit!*

But the guy had done the impossible. He was half the size of Meat Ax, and he'd put him in the ground. And then he'd busted through the blockade. And then he'd lost them.

Crater was in no hurry to meet this guy Traveler.

He and his compadres were riding along a dirt track in the Wastelands. It was night, but the moon had risen, sending long shadows like flint knives from the rocks and stunted trees.

Crater had lost the main group somewhere a few miles back. The Hungry Ones had stopped to change a tire, and when they'd tried to catch up with the main group, they'd come to a fork. Crater had taken the wrong one. He realized that, now. The track he'd taken was getting smaller and smaller.

And then, it disappeared entirely. It ran up to a little shack, and that was the end of it. Just a lonely little tin-roofed shack out in the middle of nowhere.

Crater raised his hand for a halt and slowed the bike to a stop. The Ford pulled up behind him. The Ford was stripped back so that most of the body was gone. Pieces of scrap metal were wired to the back and side windows, with spaces left for shooting. The Hungry Ones' symbol was painted garishly on the doors: an open, dripping shark's mouth. The Hungry Ones wore smudged silvery outfits they'd taken from the mummies of soldiers—long dead in their concrete bunker—they'd found farther south. They wore antiradiation suits, without the helmets, but the Hungry Ones wore them as a sort of uniform. The shark logo was painted on the back of each one.

Most of the other roadrat clubs thought they looked like real jerks.

Crater got off the Harley and signaled Merle and Berle, the two dumbest, to go check out the shack ahead of him. They snuck up to it. The windows were blocked out by dust. They kicked in the door and leaped inside, their bows and arrows at ready. Berle let fly with an arrow at a figure sitting at a card table.

Then he laughed and signaled for the others to come in. "S'okay," he shouted.

Crater went swaggering in, as if he'd known it would be safe. He looked around at the interior in moonlight from the door.

At the old wooden table two skeletons sat facing each other; they sat in straight-backed wooden chairs. Shreds of clothing and skin, gone yellow, clung to each one. Spider webs had spread through their ribs. On the table was a chess set, still set up. Looking at it in the light from a window—which Berle busted out so they could see better—Crater saw that one of the dead guys had had the other one in checkmate. There were two guns lying on the floor, one by each skeleton. There was a bullet hole in each skeleton's head.

If he'd been a different sort of man, Crater might have said: "Men when they're alone together too long begin to attach too much importance to minor triumphs."

But what he said was, "Guess one got pissed 'cause the other one beat 'im. He drew and the other saw it coming and they did each other."

Ugly Bro thought that was funny as all hell. After a few minutes of thinking hard about it, they were all laughing.

"Bro," Crater told him as he kicked a skeleton off a chair so he could sit down in it, "go out and look around. They's some hills over there, off north. Just head up the top and look around, see if you can spot some fires or lights from the others."

"But shit, Crater—"

"Okay, goddamnit, take Ned with you." The two of them went. Ugly Bro was called that because somebody'd cut off his lips and most of his scalp. Ned was a long, tall drink of corn liquor with a southern accent and black teeth. Their silver suits were pretty badly torn up. And they were crisscrossed with bandoliers.

Merle and Berle, who were twins and who looked more or less like razorback wild pigs on their hind legs, all squat and bristly and piggy-faced, stared at Crater and licked their lips.

"Yeah," Crater told them. "Go get it out. And bring it here before you open it."

They bumped into each other in their haste to get out the door, in a way that made Crater think of the Three Stooges, even if there were only two of them. Crater was old enough to remember Larry, Moe, and Curly; he was fifty-five, a grizzled remnant of the Devil's Bastard Sons, a gang out of Long Island. He'd been on a cross-country blast with the DBS when the Third One hit, and everything turned upside down. The world got to be just the way the bikers always said they'd prefer it anyway—nothing but outlaws and the Basics. Only, it turned out Crater didn't like it at all.

For one thing, it was damn hard to get parts for your bike.

And gas—shit! More than once he'd nearly got himself killed or worse when he went on gas raids. And the food. Damn. He sighed, wishing he was back in a McDonald's or a Howard Johnson's by the freeway. Maybe next door to a Shell station where you could fill up your tank without anybody trying to skin you alive for it.

Crater was short, shaggy, bearded, losing his teeth. He had only one good eye, and one of his ears had been shot off. But, he told himself, he could still get it up.

If the machinery worked, everything was okay; that was Crater's philosophy in a nutshell.

Merle and Berle returned with the big plastic cooler between them. They set it down in front of them. In it were two big jars of pickled meat—human meat, mostly. Crater had gotten used to that. And a gallon cannister of liquor, distilled from God knew what they'd bought in Drift. Traded three shotgun shells for it. They didn't have a shotgun, so it was a good deal.

Merle and Berle watched while Crater ate, stuffing the pinkish meat into his hair-rimmed mouth and chewing briefly, following it seconds later with a wash-down of the homemade firewater.

When he felt like he'd puke if he ate any more, he signaled Merle and Berle to have their share.

By the time Ugly Bro and Ned got back, they were all pretty skunked.

Ned looked excited, his skinny, dirt-blackened face jumping and twitching with suppressed information. "Hey hey hey, ya'll ain't gonna believe it, but we got us a beauty of a set-up!"

"Come on, damn it, Ned, spit it out," Crater said.

"A woman! On the other side of the hill there's a road and a busted-up building, and there's some guys in it with guns. But this girl—she left their camp! Crazy bitch looks like she's out *taking a walk!*"

Crater looked at him incredulously.

"Doing—*what?*"

"Taking a fucking *walk!*"

They all had a good laugh at that. Then Crater stopped laughing. "Maybe it's *them*," he said. "They had a girl with 'em."

"She got the pertiest blond hair I ever—"

Crater shot out of his chair—and then nearly fell over as the room spun around him. He was drunk. "That's her!" he said huskily. "Shit, we gonna get laid and get all that gold too!"

Amazingly enough—she *was* taking a walk.

Sandy was all wired up inside from the long ride, the days of just skirting death. She told herself: "It's okay— Traveler lost those creeps, and we're miles from any others. And I'll stick close to camp."

She was too restless to sit still in camp.

But there was more to it than restlessness.

She was thinking about Traveler, and she couldn't think about him, somehow, with Thorne around. She was thinking maybe she was in no great hurry to get to Kansas City. To marry some stranger, live in a strange town. Traveler was . . .

Her thoughts cut off when she heard the twigs snapping.

She remembered stories she'd heard. Stories about the packs of wild dogs. Stories about the mutated horrors who were said to live in the mountain caves, who sometimes came down and dragged people away with their impossibly strong talons.

Stories about roadrats torturing their prisoners.

She was about ten yards from the rear southern corner of the ruin where Scott and Thorne and Mortner sat around waiting for Traveler and Pearlman to return. Scott had been looking out a window when she'd left; Mortner had noted her going morosely and said nothing. Thorne was asleep, propped against a wall.

None of them knew where she was.

To her right was a turret-shaped pile of rocks that reached to about five feet above her head. The hill loomed over the turret, steep and treacherous.

To her left was a copse of some scrub bush that seemed to grow clusters of darkness instead of berries. It was barren, that scrub, but she couldn't see into it.

The sound had come from in there.

That's the direction someone would come from, she realized, if they'd circled the hill. No one had looked on the other side of that hill. There might be anything living on the other side. Maybe something that waited for passersby to wander into the ruins for shelter. Using the ruins for bait. Coming out like a trap-door spider to capture and eat whatever was there.

The moon, yellow and leering, gloated down at her.

She began to move slowly toward the ruins. She was afraid to shout, afraid to run. Something told her that shouting would bring the whatever it was down on her more quickly.

She heard another stealthy footstep and what sounded like someone panting.

She wished she'd brought the rifle. She decided to run for it. She turned, and—

The moonlight shone full on the thing's face, a face half torn away. It had no lips; most of the flesh around the mouth was missing, so that it made a perpetual skull's grin. The top of its head was a scabrous cap of red with the bone of the skull showing through in places. Its eyes were yellow and stared at her hungrily.

She bent and picked up a fist-sized rock and turned to smash it into the horror's face. But someone else clamped blackened fingers around her wrists and the one with no lips stuffed a filthy rag into her mouth and together they dragged her into the darkness.

Traveler and Pearlman passed two campfires and the humped shapes of men sleeping beside them. Others slept in tents; on bad weather days they slept in the cars.

A few roadrats sat up at the entrances to tents, smoking smash-weed, the mutant marijuana that was said to impart the effects of PCP, opium, pot, and glue-sniffing. Silhouetted by light from a campfire, a huge biker straddling one of the smaller youngsters in a plastic tent. There just weren't enough women to go around. And when the roadrats found women, they often couldn't restrain themselves from torturing them. To death. Only after the women were dead did the roadrats remember to regret their impetuosity.

The camp stank. Traveler wished, then, that his senses weren't so acute.

More than once Traveler nearly blew it by gagging.

But no one looked up as they slipped past, sneaking from shadow to shadow.

The tent containing the precious fuel was guarded by an immense roadrat puffing on a smash-weed pipe and staring fixedly into a dwindling campfire. Every so often, he giggled.

Traveler gestured to Pearlman and led him around back of the tent, skirting the circle of firelight. Pearlman slit the rear of the tent. Traveler looked around nervously as the slitting made a *zzzzip* sound. There was another fire a little further up the canyon; he could see the outlines of men sitting with their backs to him, limned in firelight. No one was looking their way.

Pearlman pressed the new tent flap back and looked through. He nodded and they crawled in. There was a man sleeping to one side. He was snoring.

They positioned the fuel bladder, found a funnel, and opened the nearest can. Gasoline. They began pouring it, Traveler holding the bladder, dripping the gas onto the side of the funnel's interior to make as little sound as possible. Still, it gurgled.

After a few minutes Traveler felt a chill of warning.

He realized that the man sleeping to one side had stopped snoring. He looked toward him. The man's eyes were open, staring at them. He was opening his mouth to shout.

Almost absentmindedly, Pearlman set down the can, drew his knife, reached over, and stuck it completely through the man's windpipe and spine, pinning him to the ground. The roadrat shuddered and lay still. His eyes remained staring—but glassily now.

Traveler looked cautiously out the front of the tent.

61

The guard was sitting with his back to them, rocking, smoking, staring into the fire, giggling.

They went back to work. The fumes in the tent made them a little dizzy.

Twenty minutes later they had as much fuel as the bladder would carry. Traveler opened the eight remaining gas cans and ran strips of cloth into each one, tearing the cloth from the sleeping bag of the dead man. He twined the turps-soaked cloths together near the dead man's head, then stuck one end in the man's open mouth. He had noticed a handful of candles in a box beside the front doorflap. He took one of the candles out and broke it into a one-inch stub, then lit it with one of his few remaining matches, saved preciously in the metal tin he carried in his pocket. He stuck the candle in the dead man's mouth beside the rags. Carefully. When it burned low enough . . .

"Let's go," Traveler whispered.

He and Pearlman, together, shouldered the six-foot plastic bladder and carried it out through the hole they'd made in the rear of the tent. It was like carrying a giant slug.

The men at the fires were noisier now, drunk and stoned.

They were singing bits of some roadrat rock-chant traditional:

Hungry Mr. Spike got a silver studded black leather hat,
He sleeps in the sewers, he'll eat only fine Persian cats,
He stands on the corner, got a sharpenin' stone in his hand
For the man who gonna stab him, his best death-dealin' man. . . .

Traveler and Pearlman moved awkwardly through the darkness, the fuel bladder shifting squishily between them. The guard at the tent's doorflap was staring into the embers. Giggling.

They kept close to the canyon walls, breathing hard, eyes burning from gasolines fumes. They reached the cars and trucks, wormed through to the horse. Pearlman took the bladder and threw it over the horse's back, lashed it in place. Traveler climbed onto the horse; Pearlman went to get another, with a bridle. He came back leading the horse, saying, "I don't know if that bit with the candle was such a good ide—"

WHUMP. Shoooosh.

Screams. Looking over his shoulder, Traveler saw men running and screaming, afire, human torches lighting up the box canyon's walls; the rough lines of the canyon walls seemed to resolve into leering faces, gargoyles laughing in the light from the howling, burning men below.

Traveler got off the horse.

"What are you *doing*?" Pearlman demanded.

Traveler said, "Just hold it a sec." He tied the horse hastily and ran to the first car, opened its hood, bent in, and with his knife, cut through wires, slashed fuel lines. He did the same with every other vehicle at this end of the canyon. He ran back to the horse and untied it. Men were running toward them, lanterns in hand, guns in other hands, shouting.

Traveler climbed onto the the horse, unslung the shotgun, and turned to face the men running between the cars at him. He let go once, pumped, then a second flash—shredding blast, and two men went down with hamburger where their faces used to be. His horse leapt, terrified by the noise, and bounded after Pearlman, who was already taking off.

Traveler nearly fell off the horse. He clamped its ribs with his legs and locked his hands around its neck. The fuel bladder sloshed under his arms.

The wind whipped past his face, the horse's mane streamed, and the yellow moon rode just overhead. He found himself grinning.

But a half hour later they were still a mile from the camp. It had been a long trudge to the roadrats' camp afoot; somehow it seemed farther on the way back, though they were riding. Maybe because Traveler's ass was sore as a bride left at the altar.

They stopped a few times and listened but heard no sound of pursuit. The roadrats would need time to repair their cars. And they had no bikes with them, that Traveler had seen; this was a separate roadrat group from the one that had pursued them with the Horde.

At last they came to the asphalt road. They followed it south a quarter mile and came to the hollow under the hills containing the ruin. There was no light or sign of life in the ruin. That's the way it should be.

They dismounted, gratefully, and led the horses into the ruin. Scott met them at the door of the little courtyard where they'd made camp. He was grinning. "You did it?" He saw the fuel bladder on the horse's back. "You *did* it!"

Traveler grunted as if to say *What did you expect?*

He tied up the horses and gave them water and an armful of the sour wild grass that grew in patches hereabouts. Then he let them go. Pearlman helped him pour the fuel into the van in the light from a kerosene lamp.

"You guys are walking kind of funny," Scott observed.

"Fuck off," Pearlman growled.

Scott had a can of food ready for each of them. They ate hungrily, squatting with their backs to the wall. Thorne and Mortner were snoring. When Traveler had finished eating, he asked, as if he didn't care, "Where's Sandy? Asleep?"

Scott shrugged. "I guess she's sleeping in your van on the cot."

Traveler stretched out on a heap of soft dirt. He was burnt. He was wasted. He was dead on and off his feet. Sleep closed in on him, blanketing the vague disquiet.

It wasn't till he woke at dawn that it hit him:

There was no one sleeping in the van. He'd have sensed them in there.

He went to look. The van was empty. She was nowhere in the camp.

7

A Dead Man Has the Perfect Poker Face

They'd been playing cards for hours.

They sat around the wooden table on boxes and overturned cabinets and chairs. There were five of them. The two brutish twins, each with his crest of mohawk bristle, his head shaved to either side of it (now and then one of them would reached up with his knife and absentmindedly scrape a little stubble from the bald part and never seem to notice when he drew blood); the shaggy one who kept looking at her with his one good eye; the tall goony-looking one they called Ned; and the one with the ripped-up face and the skull grin. Ugly Bro.

They were playing poker, and Sandy was the stakes. They were using pebbles for chips, and whoever won the pebbles from all the rest was the one who got the girl.

Got her first, that is.

When they'd dragged her into the shack, the shaggy one, their leader, had started to climb out of his silvery suit. He was going to have the first go at her. But the others had agreed that it wasn't fair that he should have everything first. He looked surprised. Evidently he wasn't used to their questioning his orders, and it worried him. So he'd thought up the card-playing scheme, and they'd agreed.

There was a can of some liquor on the table, and now and then one of them took a swig.

She was trussed with strips of leather, her hands behind her back, in the corner. They'd pawed her, but no one had abused her much; there was too much disagreement about who should be allowed to abuse her, and that had to be settled first.

Her feet were untied, but she was sprawled with her back to a corner of the dusty old shack, and they sat at the table between her and the door.

At either end of the rectangular wooden table sat two skeletons, yellowed and spider-webbed. She could see in the ribs of one a large black spider poised in its web just where the dead man's heart had been.

Everyone at the table is the same, she thought. A spider for a heart.

They'd brought out two threadbare packs of cards and stuck some cards from one pack in each of the skeleton's hands, propped on the table so they seemed to be playing.

The roadrats played an erratic game with the other set of cards, every so often stopping to argue about a hand, nearly erupting into fights.

And now and then each of them would turn to look at her hungrily.

She wished she had the deer rifle Traveler had given her. Or a machine gun. That would be nice. A machine gun and her hands free. She'd blow the bastards into stinking pieces.

One of the windows had been broken out; a window to the left of the door. She could see the sky at the horizon turning from gunmetal-blue to blue-gray. Dawn breaking.

They hadn't brought her very far. Not more than a mile. Maybe the others would come. . . .

But probably, if they came, they'd come too late.

She ached from the uncomfortable position. Her hands were numb behind her. She was both exhausted and taut with fear.

I'll make them kill me somehow, she told herself. I won't give them the pleasure of raping and torturing me. They'll have to settle for necrophilia.

Her legs were going to sleep. If she was going to force them to shoot her, she had to be up and ready to run.

"My legs are killing me," she said suddenly. "Is it okay if I stand up?"

"Don't you move!" one of the bristly twins said. "*Don't you move!* I'm gonna win you, so don't you move!"

"Shut up, Merle," the shaggy chieftain said. "Sure, you can stand up, little-sweet-thing. Get it in now. After we done with you, you gonna be too fucked-up between the legs to stand tomorra!"

She stood, slowly, and did a few knee bends to wake her legs up.

"We got to give her to the Black Rider, huh, Harley?" the one called Merle asked. "Couldn't we keep her? We could chain her up and feed her stuff. When I was a kid, we had a little puppy dawg my daddy chained up, and we fed it stuff." He scowled. "But Berle there kilt it with some gasoline and a match."

"I did not kill that dawg!" Berle retorted, spittle flying from his flaccid lips. "*You* done it!"

"Shut up, you two!" Harley commanded them. "An' yeah, we got to give her to the Black Rider. He's the one got the commission from the Glory Boys. She's the Big Prize. We get her, that stops the business between Wichita and Kansas City and the president down in Vegas is happy and maybe he'll give us a fucking medal along with the gold!"

"A medal!" Ned cawed. "Gawd-dayem!"

Sandy was looking at the door.

Maybe wait till they got a little drunker, got caught up in playing. And then go for it.

But the skull-mouthed one. He wouldn't take his eyes off her. Yellow eyes, like a coyote's. He never seemed to blink.

"Dammit, Bro," Harley Crater roared, "are you gonna stare at that bitch or are you gonna play your cards?"

Bro looked at his cards, then flicked his yellow eyes back at her. His eyes made her think of everything ugly that was yellow. Hepatitis. Nicotined fingers. Yellowed bones of the dead.

She shivered and looked away.

Ugly Bro, he of the yellow eyes, said, "Couldn't we . . . just take her clothes off? Just to . . . to look at her?"

Harley Crater frowned, considering. Then he shook his head, to Sandy's immense relief. "Nahh. I almost won it all anyway, so you'll see 'er nekkid soon enough."

He laid down his cards, saying, "Call."

The others looked at his cards and groaned. "Full house," Harley said. "Anybody beat that?"

The others threw down their cards and spat.

She thought: *Shit, this is it.*

And she bolted for the door.

A moment ago they'd been swaying in the chairs, drunk, bleary. But now they leapt to their feet. Yelloweyes was the quickest. He darted to the door, cutting off her retreat.

She backed toward a corner, looking desperately around, wishing her hands were free.

The five roadrats ambled toward her, grinning. "Don't ferget," Crater told them. "I'm first."

Traveler stood at the top of the hill, staring down at the shack a quarter mile away.

He saw the old Ford sedan out front, and the lowslung Harley-Davidson. He could just make them out at this distance, through the haze of dawn. There was a slight ground fog; the yellow earth was silvered with mist here and there; the horizon gleamed with the new sun like a white-hot blade.

Traveler was carrying the Armalite AR-180. If she was still alive, it would be necessary to shoot carefully, to excise her surgically from their midst. The shotgun was too indiscriminate, and the HK91 was too clumsy.

She was probably dead. More than likely he'd find nothing but pieces of her. But he had to try.

He wondered if he should go back and wake the others. But some instinct told him: Do it alone.

Surprise was his best advantage. One of the others might blow it.

He trotted down the hill toward the shack. His trotting became a sprint when he heard the screams, echoing thin but piercing across the flatlands below the hill.

All the way down, and across the pocked plain, he told himself: You're a damn fool for getting involved in all this.

But Christ he hoped they hadn't hurt her.

"Can me'n Merle hold her for you while you do her, Harley?" Berle was asking. He had Sandy's arms clamped in his big hands from behind her.

"Yeah. Yeah, you hold her."

Sandy kicked and screamed again, hoping someone at the camp would hear. Ugly Bro grabbed one of her legs and held it. Ned grabbed the other.

Ugly Bro had his knife in his free hand.

"Cut them jeans off 'er," Crater said. "But don't put a scratch on 'er."

"The Black Rider wants her alive," Ugly Bro said. "But did he say he wanted her . . . with no scratches?"

Crater had peeled off his silver suit. Beneath it he wore a foul, gray T-shirt and a pair of cutoffs. He opened the crotch of his cutoffs, and his hard-on sprang out like a switchblade.

He looked thoughtful at Ugly Bro's question, then nodded slowly. "I believe you're right, Ugly Bro. I believe we can hurt her a bit. Long as we keep her alive."

Sandy was seconds from vomiting. And then she heard the explosion outside. She relaxed a little, then. Traveler. She knew it was Traveler. It wasn't likely he could get her out of this alive. But at least he'd kill some of these assholes.

Crater had run to the window, his member wagging.

He shouted, "Holy shit on a wheel! Somebody shot holes in my bike and blowed it up!"

He was standing just a little too close to the window.

A hand shot through and clamped him about the throat. Another hand got him behind the head.

The four other Hungry Ones stared in shock as the hands pulled, hard, and the struggling, fuming chieftain vanished through the window. Pulled through by someone on the outside.

"Somebody *strong!*" Ned said, aloud.

Merle and Berle threw the girl aside. They and Ned went and grabbed their weapons: two sets of bows and arrows and a pistol. Ned had the pistol. Ugly Bro stayed with Sandy, beginning to lick at her neck. His tongue was as yellow as his eyes. She shrieked and kicked at him. He fell back and hit his head on the wall; he lay for a moment, stunned. She used the moment to pick up the knife he'd dropped, using the half-numbed fingers of her two hands, tied behind her, and worked it around till she could saw at her bonds.

Ugly Bro was getting up and coming at her when the bonds fell away.

At the same moment Merle and Berle were running to the door. Ned was breaking the other window so he could fire through it.

And then they all had a little surprise.

Something came bouncing into the room, thrown through the broken window. It was like a bloody, hair-matted bowling ball, at first, rolling and leaving a trail of red stickiness.

And then they knew it was Harley Crater's head, cut from his body.

Ned screamed. Merle and Berle stared.

Ugly Bro rushed Sandy—

She stuck the knife in his face. He fell back, screaming, clutching at the shaft protruding from his left cheek.

The door burst open, and they fired at it. But the man who'd kicked it open had run to the broken window. A gun muzzle poked through and fired, slicing chunks out of Merle and wounding Berle's right arm, sending both of them spinning to the floor. Ned fired through the window—at random. He couldn't see whoever it was; they'd already run around the corner of the house. How could anyone move that fast?

Ned panicked and ran out the door, sprinting for the Ford.

He made it, got in, and started it. He floored it and drove flat out at the shack.

Sandy could see Traveler through the open door, staring at the onrushing car. Traveler raised an automatic rifle, took careful aim, and fired, blowing out the windshield, and Ned's brains. The car swerved and crashed into the flaming wreckage of the Harley. Minutes later it caught fire and exploded.

But by then Traveler was already walking away, Sandy at his side. They walked up the hill.

Sandy had said, "It's okay—they're all dead in there." She thought it was so.

Traveler hadn't bothered to check. Maybe it was fatigue.

And a half hour later the van was on its way to Kansas City.

But back in that shack two figures were stirring.

Ugly Bro, for one. He'd plucked the knife from his cheek, and he was uglier than ever, but alive.

And Merle. Merle was wounded, but alive. He was

crying. Because his brother was dead. "We're gonna find that guy," he kept saying. "And do awful things to him. Bad things."

"We'll find him," Bro said. "We'll find them both."

8

"The Empty Places are Not Empty, Friend. . . ."

Traveler felt strange. He'd taken his serum and several drinks, but it wasn't helping the feeling of strangeness. So he thought about it, as he drove along the broken-up highway north to what was left of Kansas City, asking himself: What's wrong?

It was the girl, of course.

The particular way she'd taken his arm when they'd walked back to the camp. He knew what that meant. It was in the touch of her hands. The way she looked at him. She wanted him.

And, goddamnit, he wanted her.

It felt strange, to want someone. To care about them, again. It hurt a little, too. It reminded him of . . . He put thoughts of his dead family out of his mind. *Now,* he told himself, not for the first time. *Think about now. The past never was.*

She was sitting in the passenger seat. Now and then she glanced at him, and when their eyes met, she smiled.

It was the smile of a woman who'd already made up her mind.

Traveler glued his eyes to the road. It was a hot day. The sky was pale blue, laced with the thin clouds that look like drops of milk poured in water and stretched membranously. The landscape had become less barren, was flecked with greenery, ribboned here and there with streams—and not all of these streams were poisoned. They were near Kansas City.

Most of the major cities had been obliterated during the final exchange of missiles in the half hour that was all of World War III. But the newly orbited laser-defense satellite successfully knocked out a few of the incoming ICBMs—including those aimed at Kansas City and Wichita. The rest of America's defense system had been paralyzed. The antimissile missiles just didn't launch because of something called EMP. Electromagnetic pulse was something the government had known about as far back as the mid-seventies. If a hydrogen bomb is exploded a hundred miles above the continental U.S.A., a powerful electromagnetic pulse ripples out from the explosion and blankets the whole country. The pulse itself is not directly lethal, to people. But it's lethal to electronic machinery, sending a current surge through everything with circuits, burning them out, making electronic communication uniformly useless. The government had made a few extremely expensive backup systems, highly insulated against EMP—and these systems worked well enough so that the ex-western-actor president was able to get a fair number of retaliatory missiles off the ground. Still, thanks to EMP, what survived of the country fell apart, each area unable to communicate with the rest.

But the president, Andrew Frayling, unlike the majority of the citizens of the United States of America, had survived.

Traveler had heard not long ago that the guy was still alive. Frayling had gotten aloft in Air Force One shortly before the first missiles struck—and just after the EMP pulse had gone out—and escaped in the EMP-protected plane to a secret base near Las Vegas, Nevada. He had a large force of soldiers at the underground base and a special team of aboveground enforcers: the Glory Boys. The Glory Boys were dedicated to Frayling's insane hope that he could restore the U.S.A. to what it had been, mostly by using force. So far, he and his few thousand loyal troops survived. They had a vast store of supplies in their base. They'd inducted new Glory Boys and "drafted" slaves for enforced labor. But they had a long way to go. Maybe a thousand years to go.

It was Sandy who'd put thoughts of Frayling into Traveler's mind. She'd told him what the chieftain of the Hungry Ones had said: that the leader of the MC Horde had been hired, along with packs of roadrats, to stop the mission of peace between Wichita and Kansas City. Frayling wanted it stopped, Traveler guessed, simply because it was a unification plan that didn't include Frayling. But—why had he used hired MCs and roadrats instead of his own men?

Synchronicity: At the moment Traveler was thinking about Frayling, "President" Frayling was thinking about Traveler.

He didn't know that the man he was thinking about was called "Traveler." All he knew, at that point, was someone had made himself a thorn in the presidential side.

Frayling was a tall, round-shouldered man with a hangdog face, jowly and pasty. He dyed his thick hair brown and usually conceitedly refused to wear his glasses. Consequently, he stumbled over things when he walked about his office.

The office had steel walls and a translucent plastic desk inset with a holographic image of the American flag waving against a sunrise.

Hanging on the wall to the left was a holographic image of the view out the window of his now-annihilated California ranch. The image had blurred, and become overlaid with ghost images, but Frayling wasn't aware of this, as he wasn't wearing his glasses.

He decided to call in his chief adviser, Beamen, to decide what to do about this Unauthorized Unification problem. He went to the desk, fumbled for the button that would summon Beamen, thought he'd found it, and pressed down hard—putting a staple through his thumb.

He howled and capered. Beamen ran in from the next room.

"You okay, Chief?" Beamen asked. He was an owlish man with a round mouth, a round face, and thick round glasses.

"Darn it, I've gotten an electric shock from the inter-office buzzer!"

Beamen examined the presidential thumb. "That wasn't the buzzer, sir. You missed it. That was—here, let me help you." He plucked the staple out.

Frayling stuck his thumb in his mouth and sucked, pouting like a little boy. He was more and more often pouting like a little boy. Beamen suspected senility. The president was well into his seventies.

"Beamen," the president was saying, "I've got a report here that this unification mission to Kansas City is getting through. Here, I'll play it for you."

He turned toward the desk and stumbled over the wastebasket, giving out with his most fiery curses: "Ding-darn-it gosh all whammy!" He made it to the desk and began to fumble among the cassettes.

"Ah . . . that won't be necessary, sir," said Beamen, coughing behind his hand. "I've heard the report. I'm the one who gave it to you."

"Oh. Well . . . what do you think?"

Beamen cleared his throat. "If you will allow me to sum up the situation, sir: the outlaw-types we hired to stop the mission were, ah, outsmarted by an unknown man driving a black van; this man apparently had nothing to do with the original mission but simply came to its aid. The man seems to be inordinately efficient. We are making inquiries into this man's identity. . . . If you will excuse the observation, sir, it seems odd to me that you decided to hire those, ah, *transients* rather than sending in our own men. Our people are more efficient—"

"Well by golly, Wilbur, you're just not thinking politics. One day I've got to unify this country again. Before the commies beat me to the punch. We can only do so much with 'armed persuasion.' People have got to believe in us, to accept us, or we'll be putting down insurgencies all the time. That's expensive and time-consuming, Wilbur. Now, if we send our own men to stop the peace mission, the people of Kansas City and Wichita will know it and resent it. We'll have trouble with them when we finally bring them in under our wing."

"I see. And that's why you're holding off on attacking those cities?"

"That's right, Wilbur. At least, that's one reason. Now my initial strategy was to just send in our troops and announce we'd taken over for the good of the citizens of those cities and as part of our campaign to rebuild the country. But when we sent the original team in, you recall, they were shot by the men at the cities' walls long before they got a chance to plead their case. They have ignored our radio requests for their capitulation. Apparently they think of themselves as 'kingdoms' and of the old U.S.A. as 'kaput.' They are walled in and well armed. Our agents have penetrated the cities but . . ." He shrugged. "Gosh-all-dang, this spy stuff takes time! We may never be able to infiltrate enough men to change the cities' attitude to rejoining the States. We may just have to build up our fighting force some more and hit them, Wilbur. But not yet, you see, Wilbur?"

"Uh . . . I think so, sir." The president was almost coherent today, for a change. It was *almost* possible to make sense of his mishmash of strategies.

"Still, sir," Beamen went on, "I am not sure we can trust this Black Rider person to stop our mysterious man in the black van. Since all the surviving members of the mission are in this van, and since they are about to pass through the Valley of the Empty Places, we might consider sending in a special helicopter team to take them out. No one's likely to witness our intervention in that valley, sir."

The president nodded sagely. "I had something of the sort in mind myself, Wilbur. Better send in the team. And if there are, by chance, observers—if anyone at all sees the intervention—tell our boys to hunt the observers down too. Best eliminate all witnesses. . . . By the way, Wilbur, what's the latest report on our reunification effort, hm?"

Beamen sighed. "Well, sir . . . we've got three counties here in Nevada and a piece of Colorado about fifty miles square."

"Oh, well . . . we're simply understaffed. We need more men. Tell them to step up the draft. Triple it."

"Yes, sir. And I'll get you the report on this mysterious black van."

"Yes . . . the man who's driving it just might be a communist agent."

If there are any communist agents left alive, Beamen thought.

Beamen quietly left the room, wincing on his way out as he heard the president fall over his desk chair.

Traveler didn't like the looks of the wrecked truck up ahead. It was lying on its side, wheels facing away, blocking the road.

There was something about it. . . .

It was intact. It hadn't been stripped by roadrats. And yet the skeleton in the overturned cab made it look like it had been there for a long time. Someone wanted it to look that way, but they hadn't wanted to strip it. Probably because that overturned truck could be righted and driven. Because it had been deliberately overturned by its drivers, who expected him to slow or stop for the wreckage, maybe get out and look it over.

Because it was a trap.

It was only twenty feet ahead when he pulled up short, so that he and Sandy rocked in their seats.

Immediately, the savages who'd been hiding behind the big overturned freight truck sprang into the open, crude weapons in hand. They were nude except for man-hide loincloths and vests decorated with strings of man-teeth and dried fingers. Their white skin was brightly painted in red and blue lightning patterns, and their hair was teased up and lacquered into shape so that each man's coif resembled a nuclear mushroom. They were permanently stoned on smash-weed, and they came on like a pack of rabid dogs, eyes wild.

"Road cannibals!" Traveler shouted, slamming his window's metal shutters. "Cover your windows! Get onto the gun slits!"

The road cannibals had picked a devilishly ideal place for their ambush. The ground on either side of the road rose to steep slopes—the road had been cut through a hill—and there was no room to drive around. The ground on the other side of these hills was too rocky and creviced to be negotiable. The only way through was past the ambush. But how?

"Why don't you back up?" Mortner whined from the rear as the cannibals swarmed, howling around the van.

"No way around 'em," Traveler said. "We've got to go through 'em." He shrugged, cocking the forty-five. "Somehow."

"But damn it," Thorne shouted, as a cannibal bashed at the windshield with a wooden club. "They're going to get at the tires soon!"

"Mr. Traveler knows what he's doing," Pratt said with a quavering false cheerfulness.

"Shut up and let him work it out!" Sandy shouted at them.

The cannibals were carrying mostly crude spears,

slings, knives, arrows. Only their leader had a rifle. There were at least twelve of them. They ran whooping around the van, banging at it, filling it with their maddening clamor.

Traveler was waiting till they got confident enough to move in close.

He watched in the side mirror as one of them reached down to slash at a tire.

Traveler put the van into an abrupt reverse and ran over the man's wrist, crushing it. The van kept going, also crushing three road cannibals who were trying to pry open the back door, and who squealed, now, as the van's big wheels rolled over them, squeezing their vitals out and rupturing their bellies. Traveler could feel the van bump as it went over the bodies.

Traveler didn't feel bad for them. He felt a little satisfaction, in fact. There was no telling how many women and children had, along with their escorts, blundered into road cannibal traps like this one. And the road cannibals were said to tie their victims up and cut pieces off them over a period of days, slowly eating them alive.

Traveler backed over the bodies, then jerked the wheel around hard as he stepped on the accelerator so the Meat Wagon acted as a kind of three-quarter-ton bludgeon, smashing over cannibals on the van's right side, knocking through them flat, killing at least one of them. He fired through a slit in his side window at a cannibal's skull-painted face, saw it erupt in gore as the .45 slugs at close range crunched through bone and brain. At the same instant he used his free hand to steer the van for another attack angle. He shifted gears, then stepped on the accelerator, driving hard after the four who were running back to their overturned truck barricade.

He could have cut these down with the topside machine guns, of course, but he didn't want to waste precious ammo when he didn't have to.

He caught up with the last two of the four retreating cannibals, his grill plowing into one, then the other, both in the same second. Sandy looked away as the men were sent sailing broken-backed after their file-toothed comrades, to fall shattered and twitching in the road.

Traveler screeched the Meat Wagon to a halt a yard from the truck. Spears and rocks bounced from the van's snout and windshield as he backed up.

He backed up a hundred yards and stopped. He sat quietly for a moment, considering his options.

To the others, it seemed as if he were staring catatonically into space.

He was thinking: Problem—how to get around the wreck in the road. Or through it. Nothing with him that would blow it out of the way—high explosives used up. Probably the cannibals had some kind of hidden derrick affair they used to right the truck when they needed it. But finding that equipment would take time and would entail risk of being sniped at with arrows. He could attach a chain to the truck at one end and back away, try to pull it out of the roadway. But he'd have to kill all of the cannibals first. They'd probably retreat if he came after them with automatic weapons, and then they'd take potshots with arrows from the high ground. And his van might not have enough power to move the truck, anyway.

He was stuck.

84

Unless . . .

He turned to Sandy. "You know how to shift this thing, don't you?"

"Sure," she said, nodding. "Looks like a conventional gearshift."

"Okay. We've got to time this perfectly. Are you quick?"

"I was a great squash player."

"Then listen—I want you to pop it from four-wheel drive to two-wheel drive when I say *Now!* You've got to be able to do it exactly when I say. And in a tense moment. If you fuck up, we could all be dead."

"Uh—" She hesitated only a moment. "Yeah, I can do it."

They looked at each other. He realized that he could have got Pearlman to do it. But he was testing her. If there was going to be something between them, he wanted to know that she was tough and useful in a hard situation. She'd kept her head when she'd gotten kidnapped and hadn't become hysterical about it afterwards, as some people would have. But then again, she'd done at least one cotton-brained thing: She had moodily gone for a midnight walk in the wastelands, alone and unarmed.

Traveler, after years of military training, had learned to enjoy tests of skill and guts. Sometimes he got himself into a fight just to see if he could get himself out again. Just to look a challenge in the face and beat it.

He was doing something of the kind now—for both of them.

"Okay," he said. "Try it. A dry run."

She practiced with the shift for a few minutes, and

then Traveler pronounced them ready. "Everybody hold on!" he shouted.

He shifted into four-wheel drive and into first gear. He began to accelerate. They began to roll toward the cannibals, blinking stupidly at them from either side of the truck.

He shifted into second, then third, continuously accelerating.

Faster. Faster. *Faster*.

The van was screaming along at 105 miles per hour as it came near the barricade.

Pratt was holding on in the back, licking his lips and saying, "Oh, dear."

Mortner was saying, "Shit, we're gonna die, this maniac's going to smash us up!"

Thorn squeezed his eyes shut.

Pearlman lifted one of his eyebrows. That was all.

Scott held on tight and gaped, openmouthed, as the body of the big truck seemed to swell up to fill the windshield.

Two seconds to impact. One second—

Traveler swerved and ran the Meat Wagon up the eighty-degree slope at an angle of forty-five degrees from the road.

The van's front end leaped up the side like a bear trying to leap from a bear pit. The wheels whined and bit into dirt and gravel. The van climbed. Then, when it was just above the truck on the roadbed and about to pitch over onto its side, Traveler shouted, "Now!"

Sandy shifted, and the van went to two-wheel drive, the front two wheels pulling it along.

Traveler strained at the steering wheel, jerking it hard to the left. He needed both his hands—and hence needed Sandy to shift. The front-wheel drive would have been overwhelmed by the rear push; at that imbalanced point the push of the rear would have tumbled the vehicle onto its side. But with the two front wheels alone pulling *and* simultaneously angling the car to the left and down, the van shifted so that its inertia was behind it. It turned almost hairpin-tight to slam down back onto the roadway upright.

The Meat Wagon leapt and rocked on its front shocks, the axles groaned—but held. He straightened out, shouting, "Pearlman! Get a few with the—"

But it was unnecessary. He could hear the hammer of Pearlman's firing through the rear gunnery slit, using the big HK to cut down the remaining cannibals.

They whipped around a curve and left the ambush site behind. Pearlman stopped firing, and everyone started breathing again.

A few minutes later he realized that Sandy was looking at him expectantly.

He kept his voice dry and brittle as he said, "You did all right."

She smiled, and laughed. It was a soft, natural laugh. Nothing cynical or bitter or forced about it. He hadn't heard a sound like that in years. It was music. But he said, "What's so funny?"

"You are. You're *soo* cool and tough and reserved. And I don't believe any of it—except maybe the tough."

"And what do you think I really am?"

"Basically—a nice guy."

He snorted. "The nice guy who cut off that roadrat's head and tossed it in through the window?

He took his eyes off the road for a moment to see what her reaction to *that* would be. She looked a little uncertain—but not for long. "I know why you did that," she said. "To shake them up. Make them nervous, panicky. Psychology."

He nodded grudgingly. She was right. He took no pleasure in terrorizing.

He looked at her. And nodded, allowing himself to smile. Her smile was full of sun, and sex. He couldn't take his eyes off it.

It's a mistake to take your eyes off the road, in 2004 A.D. Just don't do it.

"Look out!" Scott shouted, pointing at the road.

An immense furry animal, big enough to fill most of two lanes, was sitting right smack in the middle of the highway.

"Holy shit!" Traveler blurted, swerving, and hitting the brakes.

The Meat Wagon fishtailed, and missed the fur-bearing mini-mountain, wheels protesting as it looped around the road edges. With two inches to spare on either side.

Traveler pulled up and did a U-turn about twenty yards beyond the shaggy giant. He sat behind the wheel, letting the van idle, staring. He'd never seen anything like it.

It was a Siamese cat.

It just sat there on its haunches, tail switching, gazing at them serenely with crystal-blue eyes big as headlights. It was twice the Meat Wagon's bulk. Looking closer, he could see there were a few structural anomalies in the way it was put together—a proportionately thicker skeleton, heavier legs, rougher coat. "It's beautiful!" Sandy breathed.

Traveler had to nod. It was.

"Maybe you'd better not sit there like that," said a voice at Traveler's left elbow. "He might get curious and come to look you over. . . ."

Traveler had whipped out the forty-five and was pointing it at the little man looking through the slit in his metal-shuttered window.

"You don't need the gun, for me," said the little white-haired man. "I decided already not to allow you to be harmed."

"Oh," said Traveler. "Thanks."

He lowered the gun, sensing that the old man meant no harm.

"Uh—" Sandy began, clearing her throat. " Is that your cat?"

"Uh-huh."

Traveler opened the window. The stranger was an elfish little man with bright blue eyes not so different from his cat's. He looked as if he were partly Japanese, and he was. He wore an orange robe and his head was shaved.

"I am Nicholas Shumi," said the little man.

"Traveler," Traveler said.

"I know who you are. In fact, I've seen a great many things about you. You are going to come back to this area soon, and you'll need my help. We'll become friends."

Traveler smiled at this eccentricity. Or so he took it to be. "You're a . . . priest?"

"A Priest of Buddha," the little man said, bowing. "I have that honor."

"The cat . . ." Traveler began. "What, uh . . ."

Shumi chuckled. "He likes to sit on the road because it's so warm. In most ways he is like any cat. But he is smarter than the small variety and twice as lazy. He is not a very practical cat. He is too big for his health. The gravity is too strong for him. I fear he will die soon. I have just come to fetch him home, sensing that he was . . . making problems."

"What does he eat?" Scott asked, a little nervously.

"He eats Evil. . . . His name is Ronin, which is Japanese. It means a samurai warrior, of a special kind. A sort of mercenary who takes only those causes he believes in. Like you, Kiel Paxton."

Traveler stared at him. The man knew his real name.

With anyone else this would have caused him to react with paranoid suspicion. But this man inspired trust.

"What do you mean—'he eats Evil'?" Traveler asked.

"Evil people," Shumi responded promptly. "He had two of those cannibals back there for breakfast. I'm glad you got the rest. Although for myself, I am forbidden to kill."

Traveler smiled. "With friends like Ronin, I guess you don't have to. But—you probably don't eat what he does, I figure."

The old man was thin-faced, Traveler had noted.

"No," said Shumi, shrugging.

Traveler took a bagful of canned goods from under his seat, his last stash. And—in an uncharacteristic impulse—handed it to the old man. "I think it's customary to offer hospitality to Buddhist priests," Traveler muttered.

The old man shrugged and accepted the sack as if he'd expected it.

"You need a ride somewhere?" Traveler asked.

Shumi shook his head. "No. I have Ronin to carry me."

"A mutant?" Scott asked.

Shumi shook his head. "He is the result of a genetics manipulations experiment gone . . . out of control. It was centered in the valley you are just now coming to. The Valley of Empty Places. There are a great many government buildings still standing there, almost intact."

"Yeah?" Traveler asked. "Who's in them? There must be squatters."

"No," Shumi said. "No one lives in the buildings. But the Empty Places are not empty, my friend."

9

Hell Comes to the Upper World

They watched the old man amble over to his cat, which was towering over him as he reached its furry flanks. It lowered its head obediently, and he climbed onto its neck, wrapping his legs around it, sitting on its shoulders. Ronin rose, stretched, and trotted off down the road.

"What you give that guy all that food for?" Mortner asked. "We could've used that! We're on an important mission here!"

"Shut up, or I'll leave you for the cannibals," Traveler said. "Probably more live around here."

Mortner looked at Traveler. And he shut up.

Sandy was looking at him too—smiling. "Tough guy . . ." she murmured.

Wondering himself what the hell had gotten into him, he shifted gears and turned the van around, burning rubber. For north.

They were about twenty miles farther along when the copters came.

Two of them, chopping the air close overhead.

Traveler had a bad moment. He hadn't heard choppers in years. The sound brought him back to that day in the jungle . . . in El Hiagura . . . the enormous Soviet-made helicopter rising up like an angry giant hornet disturbed from its nest in the jungle, spitting poison down at them. The yellow dust. The neurotoxins. The pain.

That bastard Vallone. He'd known. He'd *known*.

Traveler hoped his LURP buddies were still alive, somewhere. Traveler hoped that Vallone, too, was still alive. So he could have the pleasure of making him dead.

The green jungle tainted by the yellow cloud of madness. . . .

"Traveler!" Sandy shouted. "You all right?"

Traveler snapped out of it. The jungle vanished. The bleak, cracked road stretched on to the horizon ahead. And above it two U.S. government gunships—half the president's air force, now—were coming at him, side by side, the big 20-mm Graflings swiveling to take aim at the Meat Wagon.

The copters were only about twenty-five yards above the road and coming in at an angle that meant—

"Strafing run!" Traveler shouted. "Hold on!" He swerved off the road, taking a chance that the crevice he'd spotted between the high banks to one side wouldn't lead into a precipice.

He found himself on a gravel road, heading downhill —as heavy-gauge slugs smacked into the asphalt just behind.

The copters would be circling for another pass.

The road cut north and sank into a narrow valley. A quarter mile ahead he saw a cluster of government buildings, a sort of federal ghost town, dust-drifted but

93

intact. He accelerated, heading toward it full speed, hoping to get under cover.

They emerged from the ravine into a roughly flat terrain. With two hundred yards to go before they would come to the government compound. They could hear the copter behind them and above, coming in for another strafe.

Traveler watched in the side mirror till he could see the landing gear of the copters. He knew about where the copters would be, relative to the Meat Wagon, when they opened up. A little lower—*now*.

As the chatter of the Graflings started, he veered right, off the road and into the dusty flatlands, steering between boulders and stunted trees, leaving a billowing cape of dust behind which rose to blur the visibility of the pursuing choppers. Slugs long as a man's index finger and twice the width of a thumb whacked into boulders, chopped trees in half, and a couple of slugs slammed holes in the van's rear door.

Careening wildly, Traveler reached the spread of low, abandoned concrete buildings and swung into the first feeder road he came to.

He roared up the old buckled concrete alley, the van jumping at the lifted edges of road cracks, sometimes bounding all four wheels off the ground to come down with a teeth-clacking bump. The copters chuffed and beat the air overhead, like frustrated predatory birds after a fox.

One of them got a strafing angle and began to hammer slugs at the van, pinging them up the road behind it. Traveler turned sharply right, just before the strafing would have nailed him, and found himself in an immense garage entranceway leading down. It went down in spirals, along a concrete ramp, like an immense nautilus shell. He switched on his only functioning headlight and swung around and around, descending. He had no choice.

Five featureless levels down, he stopped, and listened.

Faintly, he could hear the echoing air-beat of the chopping copter blades as they hovered over the building.

If the gunships had any rockets, they might just bomb the building, bring it down on top of him. *If* they had seen which one he'd gone into. There'd been several such entrances. And they couldn't be sure of getting him that way. Probably, they'd come down and hunt on foot. And they might have a lot of men with them. More effective fighters than the average roadrat.

"What the hell is going on *now*?" Thorne asked from behind. He sounded shaken. "Helicopters now!"

"Looks like what's left of the U.S. government's got it in for your little peace mission," Traveler said. "They don't like political settlements that exclude Frayling."

"Frayling!" Thorne snorted. "As if anyone trusted Frayling! He's the one responsible for the way things are. The Russians may have attacked first—but that was only because Frayling kept playing cowboy."

"If these guys take us prisoner, you may have the opportunity to explain all that to the president in person. But I doubt they're taking prisoners. . . ." Traveler said, feeding a fresh clip into his pistol.

Sandy looked at him. "You sound as if . . . as if you think they'll get us."

He shrugged. "I think they just might. But we'll do what we—"

"Scott!" Sandy burst out, staring at the boy as he keeled over.

There was a large red hole in Scott's back. One of the copter slugs had smashed through the van's rear door. The slug itself hadn't hit him, but flak from it had sliced through his back.

Traveler climbed into the back and checked the boy's pulse. He shook his head. "He's gone."

Sandy shook her head in sad wonder. "Poor Scott. He didn't say a thing. He was trying to be"—she looked at Traveler a trace bitterly—"tough."

Traveler carried the boy's body from the van and laid it down by a concrete column at the center of the spiral ramp, in the darkness.

"We're going to leave him out there?" Sandy asked, blinking away tears. "He needs . . . a burial."

"The whole fucking world is one big burial ground. One goddamn huge mausoleum," Traveler said.

She looked sharply at him, realizing the boy's death had hurt him. He'd begun to like the kid.

Traveler turned the van around, so it faced upward, and put it in park. He turned on the interior light.

"Let's eat something. I've got to think," he said grimly. He needed a drink or maybe even a booster of the serum. He was beginning to pick up the others' lifevibes again through his overactive proximity sense. There was Sandy, erratic and high-pitched as she fought to control her emotions. There was Thorne, a churn of worrisome worries and doubts. There was Pratt. And Pearlman, low and rhythmic, steady, almost featureless. And there was Mortner, a funereal drone.

And there was something else. Outside the van. Near.

96

A tangled vibe. Something—unidentifiable. Whatever it was, he didn't like it.

He swallowed a vial of the serum, and it went away. Anyway, he couldn't feel it anymore.

On the surface, in the bright sunlight, the two choppers set down side by side in the middle of a parking lot before what had been the main administration building of the U.S. Army Genetics Experimentation Center, abandoned these fifteen years.

The first man to climb out of a copter was Major Vallone. An old acquaintance of Traveler's. The man who'd sent Traveler and his comrades into the jungle, knowing that he'd probably run into the El Hiaguran neurotoxin experiment.

But Kiel Paxton, as Traveler had been known then, was a long way from Vallone's thoughts. This renegade in the black van was—just another renegade.

Vallone was a stocky, grim-eyed man with a smug, overconfident expression and steel-gray hair.

Vallone doubted the importance of this mission. It was a waste of precious helicopter fuel and a waste of precious ammunition and a waste of Vallone's precious time. But once the president got a notion in his head, there was no getting it out.

He'd brought along eighteen men, not counting the pilots. "You men from Chopper One, take the south end. I'll lead the men from Chopper Two the other way. Walkie-talkie contact every ten minutes or if you spot the target. Let's go."

The compound was laid out in strict geometrical arrangement, a Maltese cross around the administration building, each arm of the cross made up of four parallel

97

buildings. Most of the center was underground, though Vallona didn't know that. He and his men knew nothing about this place. On their map it was marked as USG INSTALLATION 6588: ABANDONED. That was all. Frayling and Beamen knew there was more to it, but they hadn't expected Vallone to have to enter the place.

Vallone and his nine men, each carrying M 19's, updates of the M 16, fanned out and checked one building after another, finding each one echoingly empty. All the files, everything, had long ago been moved out. Vallone took up the rear of a four-man squad assigned to check out the second alley they'd come to; the other five men were in the next alley down. He noted, unconsciously, that there were discolored spots in the concrete, round yard-square areas where it seemed to be white rather than gray. He assumed there was a technical reason for this.

He didn't think anymore about it.

Until one of his men stepped into a round, discolored spot, and sank in it, screaming. And completely disappeared from sight.

Vallone stopped, staring. It had looked as if something had wrapped around the man's ankle, just before he'd gone. Had he imagined that?

Hearing the shriek, the other three men turned and ran toward the place where their partner had disappeared. One in the lead ran directly to the discolored spot and stepped into it, looking around in confusion; the man behind him ran across another.

In seconds, both men had disappeared from sight.

This time, Vallone was sure. Something had pulled them down, from below.

98

"Freeze where you are, Carter!" he shouted at the remaining soldier, who was between the death spots.

Vallone approached one and unsheathed a knife. He poked at the spot and saw that it wasn't as hard as it looked. There was a hard crust and below it a kind of pasty grit. He probed more deeply.

A long, thin gray-black hand covered in cellophane—or something organic which looked like cellophane—shot out of the death-spot muck and closed round his wrist. He felt himself pulled forward. Inexorably forward and down. The thing was *strong*.

"Carter!" he shouted desperately as he set his feet for resistance.

The soldier ran up, pressed the muzzle of his gun onto the wrist of the clinging gray thing, and fired. The wrist flew apart, oozing blue-gray pus where there should have been blood. The stump vanished into the muck. The hand still clung to Vallone's arm, as a dead spider expired while clasping its prey.

Shuddering with horror, Vallone used his knife to pry the hand loose and let it fall to the pavement, where it twitched.

The corporal and the major looked at each other once, and then they ran. They were careful about what sort of ground they ran over.

When they got to the parking lot, they stopped ten yards from the copters, staring.

A rough whitish circle was forming, even as they watched, around both the copters. It appeared from beneath like a gopher mound, but more quickly.

Vallone realized that the ground under the copters must be already undermined by these things, that they were simply completing the job. . . .

Vallone shouted at the pilots waiting in the cabs. "Take off! Get it up!"

The pilots signaled understanding and began to warm up the engines. The blades lazily began to turn. Then more rapidly.

One of the copters lifted off.

The other one stalled. The pilot swore and began to restart it. And then the ground opened up beneath it. A hole twenty-two yards across appeared as the concrete beneath the copter dissolved into pasty grit. And the big copter sank out of sight, wobbling this way and that like a sinking ship, the pilot screaming, trying to get loose. Dark gray hands pulled him from the cab and into the death spot. And then both the machine and the pilot were gone.

For good.

Traveler had made up his mind to move out. If he stayed here, sooner or later the soldiers would find his garage and check it out. He'd be trapped down here.

He reached for the ignition to start the van—and froze.

He heard a sound that made his soul ice over.

It was a rasping sound, coming from the direction of the dark garage's central column. The place where he'd left Scott's body.

The sound was a long, slow scraping. Like a body being dragged away.

He said, "Oh, Jesus." Was it soldiers who'd found another way in? He didn't think so, but he had to make sure.

Then he reached under the dashboard and found a

torch he'd clamped to the underside. He said, "Pearlman. Get up here. Cover me. Sandy, get in back." She went.

Pearlman got into the passenger seat, carrying the Armalite, which he propped in the passenger side firing slit.

Carrying the shotgun in the crook of his right arm, and the torch in his left, Traveler got out. He lit the end of the torch covered with tarry, tightly woven rags. It flared up and sent long dark shadows to do an evil disco dance with wickedly thin fire reflections on the gray concrete walls.

He moved toward the place where Scott's body had been. There was a small pool of blood, and that was all.

He heard a scraping sound—overhead. He moved instinctively to one side, and something fell just where he'd been standing. A chunk of concrete big as a basketball smashed into the floor. He backed toward the van, heart pounding, and raised the torch toward the ceiling. He saw a yard-square spot of white pasty grit in the gray ceiling and a hand vanishing into it. A gray, slick hand covered with some sort of wrinkly transparent second skin.

Another spot of white was forming, directly overhead.

He turned—and blundered into one on the floor. He fell, losing his grip on the torch. It fell just out of reach. He began to sink, pulled down by an impossibly strong suction and the wiry grip of the inhuman hand on his leg. He lowered the shotgun to blast at the hand—but he'd sunk too far, and the hand was hidden, along with his lower leg, under the grit.

And something was gnawing on his ankle.

He fought back a scream, and shouted, "Pearlman, start the fucking van and get it over here!"

He was sunk to his waist, slowing the sinking by using his shotgun butt on the hard part of the concrete, levering against the subterranean pull. Pain in his ankle. Teeth.

"Pearlman, damn it!"

The van started and angled closer. He reached up and caught hold of the door handle and shouted, "Drive! Go!"

The van lurched ahead—as a boulder of concrete fell on it from above, denting the roof and rolling off behind.

"Traveler!" he heard Sandy shout.

The door handle seemed to try to tear itself away from him. but he held on, fingers straining, feeling the bones in his hands were near breaking. And then there was a sucking noise as he was pulled free of the hole. "Stop!" he shouted.

The van stopped, and he got to his feet, looking over his shoulder. The thing that had been gnawing on his ankle was slithering headfirst into the soft spot on the floor. It had arms, but both its legs were fused together. Its head—he looked away, repelled, and put the image of what he'd seen out of his mind.

He still had the shotgun. His left hand ached like the devil. He opened the van's cab door—after disarming the booby trap—and started to climb in. Then he saw the ring of white that was half encircling the van, growing a foot a second as he watched.

"Step on it, Pearlman! Move!" Traveler shouted, leaping inside.

The van burnt rubber and climbed up the ramp, around and around the spiral. Chunks of concrete, dropped from freshly appearing spots in the ceiling, fell and struck the van glancingly. Pearlman swore, swerving to miss a big one—and then they burst out into the sunlight.

Just after the copter picked up Vallone and Carter, a call came over the walkie-talkie from the other patrol. "There's only three of us left, sir! Can you send a team in to get us? Or drop a rope, or—we're surrounded! They're closing in!"

Vallone shook his head. He switched the walkie-talkie off.

Carter stared at him, aghast.

"They're lost," Vallone said numbly. He turned to the pilot. "Back to base. The guy we were after has got to be dead, if he went underground. Mission accomplished."

"But—" Carter began. "We can't leave those guys behind!"

Vallone snarled, "Don't tell me what we can and can't do, *Corporal*."

The guy on the walkie-talkie requesting help was Captain Bromandy. A pain in the ass. Had been after Vallone's post.

At least some good had come out of this. He'd gotten rid of some competition.

The helicopter rose jerkily into the sky and headed south.

They missed by five seconds seeing the van emerge from the underground garage, to head north.

10

The Hands That Kill, the Hands That Caress

They were on a ridge overlooking the last approach to Kansas City.

Traveler was gazing at the Horde encampment below and shaking his head.

"How had they done it?

"That dirt road you put them on," Thorne said, consulting his map. "I think I found it . . . just a dotted line here . . . it doubles back and heads north. It's a shortcut for Kansas City. So they got here ahead of us . . . and they're waiting."

Traveler, Sandy, and Thorne were standing outside the van, on the ridge just off the road leading into the city. The lowlands below were pooling with shadow, flickering with campfires. Traveler guessed there must be four or five hundred of the bastards down there. More had converged from other points. "We wait till just before dawn," he said with finality. "Then we break through 'em."

"But . . . it isn't possible to get through!" Mortner whined. Traveler was in a foul mood. He lost his temper, and the next thing he knew he was standing over

Mortner, fists balled. Mortner was holding his bloody nose.

"You . . . you didn't have to hit me!" he said, backing away on his ass.

"If you'd stop *complaining* . . ." Traveler began. Then he shrugged and turned away.

Traveler started the van and backed it away from the ridge, giving it the partial cover of a cluster of boulders.

His left ankle was gnawed, but not badly; the thing had had trouble with his boots. He'd cleansed and bandaged the wound, and it throbbed dully.

"I've got to get away from this van for a while," Thorne said. "I'm getting claustrophobia."

Traveler nodded, sympathizing—in a way.

He said, "Pearlman, you see that shelf in the rock up there, above us? That's a good, defendable spot. Why don't you go up there and make camp. Maybe there's a boulder you can build a fire behind. They won't see the smoke in the dark."

Pearlman nodded and led Thorne, Mortner, and Pratt up the hill.

Mortner, still holding his bloody nose, threw a glare over his shoulder at Traveler but said nothing more.

"That was stupid of me," Traveler said. "Hitting him. I guess—that thing back there at the Empty Place . . ." He shrugged. "Got on my nerves."

"Got on your *nerves?*" She laughed wonderingly. "Man, it would've made *my* nerves climb out of my body and run!"

He smiled and shook his head. "I don't believe that. I think you're a strong woman."

"I've got a feeling that's the closest I'm going to get to a compliment from you."

He shrugged. "Do you need compliments?"

"No. I need . . . something real, Traveler." She put her soft hand to his stubbled cheek.

He cleared his throat. "Yeah. Look, I—I mean, you're—"

"Listen, forget the virgin bride stuff. I'm not a virgin. And I'm not thrilled about having to be the Official Bride."

She slid her arms around his neck and toyed with the nape fuzz.

He asked himself: *Why are you holding back?*

Shy Traveler wasn't. But he was no sucker for getting into complex involvements. This girl was apparently the symbol of unity between two armed communities. It was not in his interest to piss those communities off.

But . . .

He made up his mind. "Okay. But let me clean up, huh? I—there's a stream near here. I can—"

"You just sit here on this rock and wait. . . ." She pressed him gently to sit on a low boulder. She got an empty cannister from the van and carried it to the stream; she brought it back filled with clean, cold water.

She opened the rear door of the van—he had removed the booby traps—and went inside. He heard her rummaging in her small traveling bag. There were rustling noises. Then she called out, "Come on in!"

He climbed inside. She'd lit a candle. The room seemed almost cozy. Especially because she was kneeling beside her cot wearing nothing but sheer blue silk lingerie.

Women in the year 2004 had to be practical, had to learn to fight, to put up with privation. But they were still women.

"It belonged to my mother," she said, running a hand over the silk on her thigh. Then she reached up and began to undress him. It should have been awkward, undressing with both of them in that cramped space. But she made it easy. In a few minutes he was nude, sitting on the cot, and she was sponging him off with warm water and soap. She'd warmed the water in a battery-heated coil-cannister, a part of her traveling kit designed for hot drinks. She used a silk handkerchief to wash him, everywhere, reverently. Mary Magdalene. She washed under his armpits, between his toes, his genitals, with no embarrassment, no hesitation, no hurry. The warm soapy water, the silk, her touch, felt . . . felt . . .

For the first time in years, he relaxed.

As the rigidity went out of his muscles, his back, it flowed into his groin and hardened his manhood in her hands.

She dried him, and then ducked her head over his rigid member, enclosed it in sweet warm-wet suction-ing. He felt himself inside her. He reached down and untied the leather knot holding her hair in place, let it fall freely over her shoulders. He ran his fingers through it and thought of corn silk, of days in the country with his family, of sunlight.

She took more of him into her mouth, and he could feel that she'd learned to like the feel of the flesh in her mouth. She'd learned to enjoy it. It wasn't simply an exercise performed to please her man. She sucked as if she wanted all of that hot male hardness in her, through her, always deeper . . .

He came quickly, and she swallowed the come,

relishing it, appreciating the essence of his masculinity. She let the organ rest, let it shrink for a moment, and began to kiss him everywhere else, licking, tracing the hard lines of his muscles with her tongue.

His hands moved over her of their own volition, more softly than she would've thought possible looking at him. Impulsively he bent, lifted her easily in his arms, and laid her out on the cot. He rolled onto it close beside her, and let his hands slide beneath her lingerie. Her flesh was sticky with sexual electricity. It was like taking a drug in through his skin, a soaking-up of some biological narcotic through his pores.

Out in this wasteland, in this oversized burial ground infested with mental zombies, he found an hour's worth of pure reason to live in the exploration of her curves and her wellsprings of feminine dampness. He kneaded her breasts gently, remembering gentleness as he gave it to her, wondering how he could have allowed himself to forget the pleasure of giving gentleness.

But she wanted more than that from him. And another level of sexual energy took hold.

She spread her legs and lifted her knees; he heard a sound of damp vaginal lips parting, and—iron-hard again—he let her guide him into her. Bull's-eye. Dead center.

He plunged slowly and carefully and firmly into her, gripping her hips with his hands, pulling her to him with each thrust so she moaned with mixed pleasure and pain at the depth of his penetration. He let one thumb slide over to lift the clitoral hood and begin softly caressing the blood-filled wet pink pearl in easy circular motions . . . all the while ramming into her, his tongue entwining hers, till they were a circuit of flesh, pure ecstatic forgetfulness, and for a while the madness was far away. There was only this shared pumping, driving, probing. . . . He visualized an icy mountain underground stream thrusting through soft earth to spurt out in a hillside spring.

The van creaked on its jouncing shocks.

She said huskily, "Harder . . . don't be afraid to hurt me . . . harder . . . harder . . ." Then she screamed with joy.

That was the first time she came. There were four more like that, that night.

And Traveler came again with her fourth.

She fell asleep. Traveler lay pleasantly weary beside her, letting the night air cool him off.

He couldn't sleep. He was thinking about what she was going to ask him to do.

The eastern horizon was only just beginning to shift from black to gray-black when he rolled off the cot and made coffee in her heating cannister. He drank it black and ate a synthfood packet he'd stolen from a Glory Boys cache a few months before. It was the last of his food stores.

He brought coffee to Mortner and Pearlman and Thorne and Pratt, woke them, told them simply, "I move out in ten minutes. We're going through 'em."

He'd figured it for just before dawn because that would be when they'd be least alert.

He checked the topside machine guns and made sure their drums were full.

Sandy woke, hearing the activity outside the van, and came out to ask, "Can I help?" He smiled at her. Not *too* warmly—Thorne was watching. "Not just yet," he said.

"Thorne," Traveler said, "can you signal the city somehow? Maybe they can help us get through."

Thorne shook his head. "We lost the radios to the marauders. And the city's gate-watchers will be expecting us to come in a different car."

Traveler frowned. "So if we make it through the roadrats, we might be shot down at the gate."

"Surely they'd have the sense," Pratt said, "to see that we're friends!"

Thorne shook his head. "The city is an armed camp. They're paranoid of everyone."

Traveler said, "Until I can think of a better plan, Thorne, you and Sandy make a short note stating your identity and business. I'll attach it to a crossbow bolt, try to fire it into something other than a human being on top of that gate."

"God help us if they don't move fast on it," Thorne said.

Mortner scowled and muttered but said nothing. Now and then he gingerly touched his swollen nose.

The caravan got into the Meat Wagon, and Traveler set out.

Moving slowly, the van picked its way among the rocks and potholes in the old dirt trail they'd taken up the ridge's back. The light was sparse, but Traveler didn't want to alert the roadrats by turning on his headlight.

At the bottom of the trail, where it turned toward the flatlands that lay between them and the city gates, Traveler stopped to look at the sketchy map he'd made of the area the day before.

There was just a half mile between here and the city gates.

This had at one time been part of the town's suburbs. The suburbs had been burned out, looted, and stripped in riots; the ecological disruptions that had turned much of the state into a dust bowl had done its work here too, leaving almost nothing of suburban Kansas City standing. There were a few crusts of building walls, mazelike stretches of ruins. That was all. Most of the flatland was simply dust and rocky ground.

To the east there was a sort of crevice in a low hill that formed the border of the lowlands on that side. It was dark and misty in the crevice.

Near the city, roadrats had formed a rough barrier of cars and hastily erected roadblocks of scrap wood in a U around the gate. There was a back way into the walled city, but Thorne—who had been here on a diplomatic mission before—assured him that it was too far away to reach with the small amount of fuel remaining to them. And it was probably guarded by another arm of the scum Horde.

The weakest link of the roadrat chain around the city gate was on its eastern side, near that crevice. Traveler would have to do a wide circuit of the camp, under cover of the ruins, and then try to break through at the weak point in the line of defense. The roadrats were expecting him to come from the southeast and had reinforced most strongly to protect the southeast approach.

Mortner, Thorne, and Pratt were arguing in the back about the best way to proceed.

"Someone should sneak in," Mortner was suggesting.

"Sneak through the lines and get to the gate and knock to be let in and then ask the city to help them with force of arms—"

"Knock on the door!" Pearlman said scornfully. "Are you volunteering to be the one to go, Mortner?"

Mortner turned pale.

Under cover of this chatter, Sandy, sitting beside Traveler, reached over and took his hand. She whispered, "There's another way. We can unload these jerks and leave here. Maybe head for Canada. They say there's some forest still standing up there. . . ."

He sighed. He'd been expecting this. He shook his head. "To unload them would be . . ." He shrugged. "They'd get snuffed before the day was out. *By something.*"

She made a gesture of indifference. "So what?"

He hesitated, then nodded ruefully. "I know what you mean. But I can't do it. I've got to feel like I'm . . . at least one step above animal. Anyway . . ." He glanced into the rear of the van. They were all still arguing there. Except Pearlman, who seemed to be listening to the argument with quiet amusement. Traveler looked at Sandy and whispered, "I thought about it. Already. You're . . . you made me feel like . . . like it was worth it, being alive. . . . But. You'd be killed, sooner or later, out there. I just couldn't handle that."

"You mean you're scared of me."

He turned away from her and put the van into gear. "Call it what you like."

She let go of his hand.

The sky was beginning to go pearly-silver and gray-blue. They could see the walls of the city, all built within the last fifteen years of concrete blocks, stone, and hardened earth, all scavenged from the buildings that had emptied as the city's original inhabitants had fled, mostly into death, trying to escape the fallout. But Kansas City and Wichita had been lucky. The wind had been right, prevailingly helpful, and only a small amount of fallout had fallen on the area. The city fathers attributed this to divine providence and had established what was known as the Crown's Protestantism as the official and required state religion of the city. There were no atheists in Kansas City—not in public, anyway. It was a jailable offense. The Third World War was, here, considered to have been God's judgment on a world that had lost touch with traditional values. The man with the most power in the town—of those who'd remained, some one hundred fifty thousand—was an aficionado of middle ages lore, and after he'd gone a little mad after the war, he had enforced a feudal life-style on the city's inhabitants, establishing his closest associates as knights who governed particular parts of town, and to whom the inhabitants were to vow feudal allegiance—or die.

The baron's name was Moorcock, and his power obtained from the fact that he had been an organized-crime boss. His men were loyal to him. And he had a large store of gold socked away. And he had a small army of Enforcers. Like many organized-crime leaders, he'd always secretly yearned for respectability. He found it, in a way, after the war. His protection racket was legitimized by becoming an essential part of the government. He now simply called it taxation.

And in a way, it had worked. The city was clean and even boasted running water (though not hot water, for most—too much power drain) and electricity. At least there was electricity for three hours a day, for the average person, if he paid his power taxes. (Naturally, the "aristocracy" had all the electricity it needed, as well as hot water). There were a few small oil wells around the city, and an oil-fired power plant, together with solar power, provided the city's lights on its main streets and electricity for other things, though most of the population used candles at night. Oil and gold and food from the city's underground hydroponic gardens, worked by "serfs," were traded to people on the outside for other goods. Water was sometimes in short supply, and sometimes tainted. Attrition and vandalism by roadrats and other wasteland manimals was a constant problem. And then there were the wars with Wichita over a few of the wells.

From where he sat, Traveler could almost imagine the city a medieval fortress. The outer walls resembled one. The city's skyscrapers had mostly fallen or been cannibalized, replaced by eccentric towers, walkways, crowded warrens of marketplaces. Pennons flew from the highest towers; torches lit the battlements.

Traveler began his assault of this fortress and the barbarian Horde surrounding it.

The Black Rider was truly black. Not black like an African. There was nothing Negroid in his features. He was a mutant. He was jet-black, everywhere, including the palms of his hands and the bottoms of his feet and both thin lips of his expressionless mouth. There were no whites to his eyes, and no iris. His eyes were entirely black, like orbs of onyx. He had no hair, not even eyebrows. He had no ears; in place of them were membranes which vibrated visibly when there was a loud noise near him. But, except for this, and except for a powerful proximity-sense much like Traveler's, he was ostensibly human. A dissection would have revealed that his organs were all quite human—and not black. His blood was as red as any man's.

But there was another way in which he was not human.

He had no shred, no trace, of human warmth, of camaraderie, of identification with others. Sometimes he had women. Sometimes he kept them for days—before he killed them.

He had a vast horde of MC riders who followed him everywhere. Not out of loyalty. It was impossible to be loyal to so soulless a man. They followed him because he never failed to lead them to fresh victims, to success. This problem with Traveler was his first setback.

The Black Rider called Squid, his second-in-command, to his tent. Squid stood before him, averting his eyes. "Yeah, Rider? What's up?"

Squid was a gangly, skull-faced man, his face pocked by radiation sickness. Like the Black Rider, he wore black leather, head to foot.

"Squid," said the Black Rider in his toneless voice, "I have decided something."

Squid waited. Whenever the Black Rider said that, something ugly was about to unfold. Last time it had been a purge. The Rider had decided some of his men were conspiring against him, so he'd had them taken and skinned alive, and worse.

"I have decided that we are going to ignore the orders of Frayling, in at least one respect. He wants us to leave the city alone after we get this Traveler. But I have decided that the city can be taken. Taken apart and squeezed dry."

Squid smiled. "When?"

"We hit it tonight. After we get Traveler—oh, by the way: I sense this Traveler approaching from the east. Alert the Horde. Kill him."

11

Triumph and Treachery Beyond the Wall of Blood

"Goddamnit," Traveler muttered. "Looks like they're ready for us."

He stepped on the gas.

The Meat Wagon roared out of the ruins, lifting its front wheels off the ground, coming down with a thump, bouncing, rushing on harder and faster than ever, cutting a straight line for the enemy.

The barricade, at this point, was only a chain of cars end to end, and Traveler thought he saw a place where he might break through. A gap just wide enough between two stripped-down semi-truck cabs. He angled for it, one hand reaching for the Fire button that would set off the machine guns on the roof mounts.

He was still fifty yards from the blockade when four black hawgs roared toward him, two on each side, shotguns booming; the blasts rang on the metal-shuttered windows. Another spray of buckshot was deflected by the chain mail over the tires. Traveler jerked the wheel hard left, using the Meat Wagon to ram a bike riding close beside him, slamming it in the gas tank, puncturing it with his spiked bumper; gasoline spurted onto the biker, catching fire from sparks as the metal of the bumper ripped at the bike. The man howled and the bike fell behind. Traveler glimpsed it in his side mirror—a flaming man riding a black, burning Harley, wind whipping the flames behind him. He looked like a prewar windshield decal.

And then the bike exploded, taking the one beside it along in the blast; they rode side by side into hell.

But then, Traveler reflected as the barrier loomed up ahead, this is hell. So they must be riding to something worse.

Sandy was using the rifle through a firing slit on the right. It jerked against his shoulders, and another biker went down, headfirst, the bike and momentum dragging him mouth open through the dust for five yards, scraping away his face and ramming the wasteland down his throat.

Pearlman took out the fourth with the heavy assault rifle, firing from the rear. The man tossed up his arms and spurted blood from his shattered head in an arc behind him, riding along for six yards with blood streaming through the air like a red pennant, and then the bike went down.

Just ahead four men fired at them from behind a roofing-tin barrier. This was the place, the weak lir'. of seven feet between the two semis. Bullets whined off the roof of the van as he squeezed the Fire button for the topside guns. The machine guns rattled, strafing up the ground between the van and the barrier, little spires of dust jumping in a connect-the-dots sequence till the slugs began to hammer through the sheet metal, tearing two of the men standing behind it into bits and pieces, bloody hunks flying like red flowers tossed from a basket at a wedding—the wedding of steel-jacketed death and human flesh.

"Hold on!" Traveler shouted. "We're busting through!"

"Oh my gosh!" Pratt said.

"Shut up, Pratt!" Thorne said, hiding under the cot.

"We're all going to die!" Mortner moaned.

And then the van impacted with the thin barricade, knocking it aside like a bull knocking a cape away from a slow matador, plowing through, grinding a man who was too slow to get out of the way into a mishmash of crushed flesh and splintered bone and gristle.

The Meat Wagon's underside was splotched with—meat.

Traveler pulled up short, wheels squealing in protest. He realized he'd been set up.

An old school bus, big, armored and bristling with spikes, was pulling up from the right, cutting directly in front of him. He looked in the side mirror—another big vehicle was cutting him off behind. He was boxed in. Trapped.

And the roadrats were swarming over the buses, between the trucks, coming at him, howling with glee.

He let the ones in front get between him and the bus, then he stepped on the gas and rammed them into the side of the bus, impaling them on its antipersonnel spikes. He backed the Meat Wagon hard into the ones swarming from the rear, smacking into four of them, knocking them dead or senseless, as Pearlman opened up on others, moving them down.

"I'm running short of ammo!" Pearlman shouted.

"Thorne!" Traveler yelled. "Take Sandy's place with the gun! Sandy, get behind the wheel. Drive the wagon through when the way's clear!"

119

He started to get out of the van.

"What are you doing? Are you crazy?" she shouted over the clamor as the roadrats swarmed around the van.

"Shut up and do it!" he shouted. He gave the Fire button on the steering column a last squeeze as a clutch of roadrats, wearing scraps of leather and metal lashed together, happened to run into the kill-zone. The dual killing engines minced them, made them dance as it cut them apart—and then the drum was empty.

Traveler grabbed up the shotgun and his pistol. He stuck the shotgun through the firing slit in the metal-shuttered windows and let go. The gun recoiled bruisingly hard against his shoulder as it belched blue smoke and a fist of pellets which spread to tear away faces, punch into guts, puncture eyes. Half a dozen roadrats fell back screaming.

Traveler used the moment to open the door and leap free of the van. He pumped another round into the shotgun's chamber, then crooked it in his right arm as he leapt over the still-smoking corpses of the men he'd just blasted, dodging between leering roadrats. Their faces were like smudged, psychotic circus clowns, wildly painted, hung about with bits of old transistors for jewelry, their scalps bisected by Mohawks, their eyes mad with smash-weed and black market amphetamines.

Two of them came at him from either side and tried to slash at him with hooked blades chained to metal hafts. The cycle-sickle, the weapon was called, or cy-sick or sick-stick. The crescent blade, razor-sharp, swinging in short circles on the chain-and-ball swivel attachment, whirred and caught the morning sun, slicing at Traveler's throat.

Traveler ducked, and the blade from the one on the right caught his compadre in the right eye. The man bellowed and staggered back, the skullbone of his eye socket jerking the cy-sick from his partner's hands. Traveler shot an elbow into the Adam's apple of the man who'd lost his stick, sending him gagging backward, spitting blood.

Four others were closing in. Traveler cut down three with three quick pistol shots, delivered in a second and a half with the gun in his left hand. He could have cut down the fourth that way, but bullets were too precious to waste. So he coldcocked the guy with the pistol and ran past him before he'd hit the ground.

He'd gained his objective: the bus.

Three roadrats were squatting on the hood of the bus's snout. One of them was drawing a bead on him with an arrow.

Moving impossibly fast—it seemed to the roadrats—neurotoxin-sharpened reflexes working overtime, Traveler smacked the butt of the pistol down onto the arrow, a modified karate slice catching it two feet from his chest, breaking it in half. The arrow fell in two pieces at his feet.

The roadrats stared, amazed. Their shock gave him a moment to raise the shotgun and let them have it. All three went over backward in the blast, caught in a double spread at gut level. He ran past them, firing the pistol at the two men at the door to the bus; one had been the driver.

Had been, because now he fell with a bullet hole between his eyes. The other's head jerked back as a forty-five slug caught him in the teeth. They were still falling as Traveler bounded over them and into the bus;

it was empty. The other roadrats were on top or lying where he'd killed them. He twisted the ignition, at the same time looking at the Meat Wagon. Sandy was jerking it back and forth, using it to ram at the attackers. The "bulletproofed" front windshield had begun to crack. It would go in another few seconds.

And the fucking bus didn't want to start. The engine whined, but wouldn't turn over. A roadrat appeared in the door, leveling a shotgun at him. Traveler reached over and jerked hard on the lever for the bus's folding doors, slamming them shut in the roadrat's face as the man fired. The door absorbed most of the shotgun blast and deflected it back at the gunman so he twisted away, mewling with pain.

Traveler twisted the key in the ignition again. The engine turned over. He shifted gears, and the bus moved ahead, out of the way. Up ahead he saw a great swarm of roadrats coming at him, removing from other positions on the barricade to reinforce this one. He opened the side door, and lashed the steering wheel into place. Then he laid a chunk of scrap metal on the gas pedal and jumped free of the bus. It picked up speed and sped directly into the heart of the onrushing mass of thugs, grinding them under or smacking them aside, catching others on its spikes.

He turned toward the Meat Wagon as it roared through the newly opened space and pulled up beside him. Traveler shot three roadrats who were clinging to the van's roof and climbed in the side door. Thorne was slumped over the dashboard, an arrow through his neck, shot through the window slit. Pratt lay beside him, a bullet through the side of his head. He'd got it while trying to help Thorne. Pearlman was firing single shots through the rear firing slit.

Mortner was hiding under the cot.

Traveler irritably nudged the bodies aside so they fell in the back, then slid into the passenger seat. But the survivors of the roadrat reinforcements were not on the trail of the van now, and two of them were jogging toward them with hand grenades. And seven bikers were riding in circles around the van.

And the city gate was still five hundred yards away.

"Christ," Traveler said. "What a bitch. They're fucking up my wagon."

He stuck the shotgun through a firing slit and let go two more rounds, knocking a dark knight off his cycle and punching a fist-sized hole through the belly of a roadrat with a grenade. The man fell back, and the grenade exploded among his fellows, dispatching three of them.

And then the ring closed around them. Traveler was nearly out of ammo. He figured this was it.

Something big and tan-colored loomed up in his side mirror. He stared. He caught a glimpse of a crystal-blue eye big as a headlight. And then Ronin was among the roadrats, spitting and hissing, the fur on his back bristling. The old man in the saffron robes hung on, legs locked around the enormous cat's neck. Shumi's face was sedate and amused; he looked like a child riding horsey. Now and then he bent to whisper suggestions to the cat.

One of the cat's paws—each pad about two feet wide—flicked down to catch a roadrat on the side of his head, snapping the man's neck instantly. With another paw it slapped down a circling biker as if stopping a scurrying mouse.

It swept three others out of the van's way, and Sandy accelerated, burning rubber through the gap, tooling hell-bent for the city's gates.

Traveler opened a window shutter, took out his crossbow, and shot the bolt with the note on it up at a flagpole atop the city's walls, but at the moment he pressed the trigger the van hit a pothole and bounced, jerking his hand so the shot went wild, the arrow bouncing off the wall.

"Dumb idea anyway," Traveler muttered.

But, up ahead, the city's huge blue metal gates were opening.

Traveler looked in the rearview mirror and saw the man in the orange robe riding the cat back the way it must have come, into that fog-filled crevice to one side of the battlefield. The cat was moving a little jerkily, as if wounded. It vanished into the fog.

And the Meat Wagon vanished into the city. Kansas City, 2004.

12

You've Seen the Triumph, Now Here's the Treachery

"I don't know what I expected," Sandy was saying in a flat, tired voice. "A ticker tape parade maybe. Not this, anyway."

There was a crowd of men in leather and chain mail around the van. Each man had either a gun or a crossbow, and each one was pointing his weapon at the Meat Wagon.

"They're not sure who we are," Traveler said.

He raised his hands to show he had no weapons in them, then bent to shout through the slit in the steel-shuttered window. "We're here from Wichita. We're all that's left of the peace mission! This is Sandy—"

"Sandra Benison," she whispered.

"Sandra Benison! She's here to . . ." He winced, then forced himself to voice the absurd. "She's here to marry the baron's son."

A tall, bearded man in a silver helmet shaped like the grill of a Chevrolet stepped up to the van, pushing authoritatively through the surrounding men. He unholstered a pistol and pointed it at Traveler's head.

"Now explain quick," he said, "what you were doing out there."

Traveler's temper was fraying. "Fighting your enemies. You'd have been out there doing it too if you weren't such a pus—"

"Excuse me, sir!" Mortner broke in, loudly. "I'm the only surviving official of the Delegation from Wichita to Kansas City. We ran into bad luck on the way."

"Bad planning," Traveler said.

"And we've just been trying to break through the roadrats barrier—"

"You say you're with the Wichita delegation?" the official asked doubtfully. "But they were coming in trucks, with an escort of—"

"They're all dead," Traveler said. "If you're so suspicious of us, why'd you let us in?"

The man with the beard scowled. "One of our gate guardsmen, Pinchello, did it. He said he saw the Top Cat coming to help you . . ." He shrugged. "A lot of people here are superstitious about that cat and the old priest. He said it was a sign, and he let you in."

Traveler shrugged. Mortner bellowed over his shoulder, "Uh, I'm Bill Mortner, acting chief of the Wichita delegation—"

"Miss Benison!" the bearded man broke out, staring at Sandy. Her hair was in disarray, her face smudged and scratched. "I didn't recognize you at first. But I see it now. It's you."

"Yes, it's me," she said dully. "Thanks for the confirmation."

"I am Count Vorsoon," said the man with the silver helmet and the big red beard. He looked at her as if expecting recognition. She stared back.

He shrugged and turned to the soldiers standing around the van. "Is that gate secured?"

"Yes, sir," said one of the men.

"Then get these people to the Third Tower; see that they have everything they need. The lady must have the best room."

"Where am I going to put my van?" Traveler asked. "It's got to be somewhere safe where I can keep an eye on it. In fact, I'll stay in it. I just want my pay, and I want to get out."

"Pay?" Vorsoon blinked.

"The man's a mercenary," said Mortner contemptuously. "He has already been paid—in ammunition."

Traveler turned and snarled at Mortner. "What the *fuck* are you trying to pull? You wanna *live*?"

"You hear?" Mortner squealed. "He threatened my life! Furthermore, he's made advances on the new bride and tried to convince her to run off with him! I heard him planning it!"

"What?" Traveler's temper snapped. He turned and grabbed Mortner by the throat. All these people, this claustrophobic environment, had got to him. People vibes, shapes, smells—an assault on his neurotoxin-frayed senses.

"Traveler!" Sandy shouted. "Wait! I'll explain—"

Mortner had twisted free. "Don't listen to her explanations! She's in love with him! If you want the ceremony to come off, you'd better eliminate this man at once!"

The side door wasn't booby trapped just then. Vorsoon jerked it open and half a dozen men dragged Traveler out. Traveler turned to the nearest, jerked his arm loose, and knocked the man stone-cold *out* with an uppercut.

But then darkness came crashing down on him in the form of a club cracked against his right temple.

It was a kind of relief.

Traveler woke in a cell.

A rose-tinged light poured through the barred window opposite his cot. An old iron door, which he knew would be locked, was the only feature of the concrete wall to the right.

His head didn't hurt—until he sat up. And then the lump laughed loudly at him with pain.

He waited till the echoes of the hurting laughter died down, and then he looked himself over. Weapons: gone. Except his steel-toed skinhead boots. No other damage to his body. Except that his nerves were shot to hell. He needed the serum.

Then he remembered the throwing stars hidden in his belt slits.

He felt the slits—and smiled. The stars were still there.

There was no door slot to push food through. Sooner or later they'd come in to feed him. It wasn't likely they'd let him starve, or kill him. He was a valuable commodity. The city sold convicts as slaves to people outside their walls.

So he'd wait till some jackass blundered in. He'd off him with a star, and his partner if he had one. . . .

There wasn't long to wait. The door's lock creaked and squealed.

Traveler took a ninja star from his belt, and then a second, holding one in each hand, composing himself for a killing throw—which wasn't easy with his head throbbing and his nerves twanging.

The door opened. He raised a star over his head, started to fling it—and at the last moment turned it so it'd miss its target. It sank into the plaster frame of the door.

He'd just missed putting the ninja star through Sandy's forehead.

She stepped into the room, accompanied by Vorsoon. Vorsoon gaped at the steel star, two of its points buried in the plaster.

Sandy looked from the star to Traveler, her mouth open. And then she laughed. "It's okay, man. Friends."

Traveler shook his head.

"I haven't got any."

"Drop that weapon immediately!" Vorsoon said, pointing to the other ninja star.

Traveler shook his head. "I've been fucked with enough. This is it. You let me go, or I take as many of you with me as I can."

Vorsoon reached for his gun.

Sandy hissed impatiently and pushed the gun aside, going to stand close to Traveler.

She looked into his eyes—and he lowered the ninja star. But he didn't put it away.

"The roadrats are attacking the city," she said. "Apparently they found out that a large part of the city's militia is away protecting a trading shipment. The men remaining . . . well, a lot of them saw your fight this afternoon. You're admired, it seems. And they saw the Top Cat fight for you. They're reluctant to fight . . . until you're there to lead them."

Traveler raised his eyebrows, looking at Vorsoon.

"I'm surprised your baron doesn't simply threaten them with execution."

"He did," Vorsoon rumbled. "But the palace guard was sympathetic to you . . . and so was the executioner. Apparently there's some legend that's sprung up about a man coming to save the city who is brought us under the protection of the cat. The old man Shumi spread the story.

"Still," Vorsoon went on. "If this lady hadn't made an appeal to the baron's son for you, you'd still be locked up in here. The baron doesn't like to give in to whims of the serfs."

"Where's Pearlman?" Traveler asked.

"He's on the wall," Sandy said. "Fighting."

Traveler heard the sounds of a battle floating distantly through the window now. Gunshots, screams, the roar of attacking roadrat vehicles.

"And where's Mortner?" Traveler asked, his voice chilled steel.

"That's none of your concern," Vorsoon said gruffly.

"That son-of-a-bitch lied—" Traveler began.

"I told them," Sandy put in.

"I want what I was promised. And I want full repairs on my van."

Vorsoon sighed. "Yes, yes. All of it. The princess has asked for it. You shall have it."

"And now," Traveler said, "I want a meal, my serum, some aspirin—and my guns. Then we get to work."

"You've got spies in your city," Traveler said.

He and Vorsoon were on the battlements overlooking the front gate. It was dark. The torches flickered and trailed sparks in a breeze. Fires winked back from the Black Rider's encampment below.

"Spies?" Vorsoon said, looking at Traveler. "Of course we've got spies. Everyone has spies. Spies from Wichita, Oklahoma City, New Settlement . . . perhaps others."

"Spies from the Glory Boys," Traveler said. "The president's people. Frayling's."

"Frayling?" Vorsoon frowned. "What makes you so sure?"

"Those people"—he gestured toward the scores of campfires like a handful of hot coals strewn across the black carpet of the flatland—"were sent here by Frayling. He didn't want you people to know he was trying to stop you. Tried to make it look like a roadrat effort. But we had the word from some of them, on the way here. Sandy was kidnapped . . . she heard them talking."

"Madness! We have a peace treaty with Frayling! We refused to let him govern us, but we agreed not to fight his men . . . as long as they kept their distance."

"You think it's natural for all these roadrats to be working together? Not on your life. The Glory Boys are behind it. The 'rats knew the route of the caravan. They had military weapons, some of them. They were onto the whole thing. Some spy or spies here set this up. Spies for Frayling."

Vorsoon looked at him suspiciously. "Why are you telling me this?"

Traveler hesitated. "To help you. Maybe for Sandy. Maybe so somebody, somewhere, can get started again. I guess it'd be a good thing if you people and Wichita united. Policed the land in between. I can't stick around to be part of a thing like that. But I like to know somebody's trying it."

After a moment he added, "Probably won't work, though."

"What?" Vorsoon's brow wrinkled. "And why not?"

"Because this feudal, royalty business—it's such bullshit. These people are Americans. They'll never stand it long. It's not in their genes, man. They just put up with it now because the war was a big shock. They like the orderliness of the place. But they'll cut your throat in your bed one night."

Vorsoon swallowed and reached under his beard to clasp his throat.

Pearlman walked up, then, the Armalite in his hands.

"So the way I got it," Pearlman said, "they attacked at this gate in two waves. We held off those two, but they damaged the gate, and next time it'll come down. We've got more men now, though. Now that you're here."

"They getting that gate reinforced?"

"Yeah. . . . But I heard a few roadrats sneaked through when the top door bolt broke. Maybe six. We got four of 'em, but—"

"We haven't got time to worry about two roadrats sneaking around the city," Traveler said, shrugging. "We've got to set up a defense against the ones outside."

And no more was said about the two roadrats who'd slipped through.

Merle and Ugly Bro were crouching under a bridge column like a couple of trolls. They were staring up at the big, Disney-ized version of a castle called the Baron's Towers.

"What I figure," said Ugly Bro, "from all I heard 'em

132

say, is that they got to be in there. Because that bitch, she's in there. The guards said that, right?"

"Yuh," said Merle.

"So he's in there too. Right?"

"Yuh," said Merle, again.

"So we got to wait till the right time and go in and find 'em both and kill 'em. Right?"

"Yuh," said Merle. And he added, "Could we do it soon, Bro? Okay?"

"Soon, Merle. We'll get the bastard that did this to us. That killed your brother. That offed our boys. Soon."

13

The Black Rider Rides In

"Looks like they're massing," Traveler said, lowering the binoculars. "They're coming at us again. I figure maybe ten minutes."

A respectful group of archers, gate guards, and militia officers stood around Traveler, watching him with awe and annoying him immensely.

He raised the binoculars for a second look . . . and he saw his Enemy.

One look, and he knew the man was his enemy, his particular Enemy, his special adversary, his personal devil.

He was looking at a man straddling an idling low-slung hawg at the point of the massing attack force. A man made out of darkness. Black eyes, no whites. No ears. A mutie. The Black Rider. Traveler had heard of the Black Rider; and the Black Rider had heard of Traveler. The Rider seemed to sense Traveler's scrutiny. He looked his way, and Traveler had the chilling sense that the Rider was looking directly *into* the binoculars . . . and into Traveler's eyes.

With a shiver Traveler lowered the field glasses and

handed them to Pearlman. "You see that mutie at the head of the bunch? The black thing? I don't mean black like African I mean black like *black*."

Pearlman looked and nodded. "Uh-huh." He lowered the glasses. "I know who he is. Bad customer. Said to have mutie powers."

"Maybe we could pick him off. . . ." Traveler turned to Vorsoon. "You got a sniper's rifle? Long-range scope?"

"No. I'm familiar with our armory. Nothing of that sort. We have a few M 16's. M60's. But we're keeping them for emergencies."

"What do you call this?" Traveler demanded.

"Maybe you're right. I'll order them broken out."

"What about artillery?"

"Ah. No. Except for a few small things. Mortars, I think they're called."

"Bring 'em out. And whatever shells you have. How many men you got?"

"Perhaps two hundred trained men. We could draft the serfs, but most of them don't know how to fight. They'd run and hide."

"I'm not so sure about that. Round up as many as are voluntarily willing to fight. Don't press 'em into it, or they'll frag us."

"Very well." Vorsoon bowled off.

Traveler turned to the Captain of the Gate Guards, Pinchello, a man with large bright eyes and a wide white-toothed grin, reminding Traveler irresistibly of Eddie Cantor movies he'd seen as a kid. "Pinchello, did you send that scout through to get the militia back to town?"

"Yes, Esteemed Knight of the Black Van, Mister

Cat-Loved sir, we sent him, only a few hours ago, out the secret gate, and with luck—"

"I've got a feeling," Pearlman interrupted, "he didn't get far." He pointed. They looked.

A roadrat pickup, lit with torches, was driving up to the gate, and mounted on its roof was a man hanging by his arms from a scaffold made of scrapwood. He swung, shrieking with pain, as the truck jerked to a stop. Traveler looked closer. The man wasn't hanging by his arms, precisely, but by hooks in the muscles of his arms, which had been cut free of the flesh containing them. . . .

Both his eyes had been cut out. And he bled from a dozen other places. He was stripped nude, so every bit of the mangling could be seen.

A Kansas City guard brought Traveler the first of the mortars, sent from the armory below.

Beneath the wall a man with his face painted to resemble a skull was standing up beside the dangling prisoner to speak through a bullhorn.

"I wonder where he got the bullhorn? . . ." Traveler murmured.

"Scavenging and looting," Pearlman said, setting up the mortar. "The Black Rider has a nose for finding what's useful."

"We will spare the city" boomed the voice from the bullhorn, "if the city surrenders now! We will not kill you all if you surrender now! Open the gates and open your coffers to us! We guarantee your safety! Otherwise you will all end like this man!"

Pinchello frowned. He turned to Traveler, asking, "Great Knight of the—"

"Can it," Traveler said.

"What?"

"Call me Traveler. My name is Traveler, okay?"

Pinchello grinned. "A great honor, Cat-Loved sir! Ah, Lord Traveler, do you think they are sincere? They won't hurt us? If we surrender?"

"They lie," Traveler said, adjusting the mortar. He nodded to Pearlman, who dropped a mortar rocket into the launcher tube.

"We must have your answer *now*—" boomed the bullhorn.

The city's reply came in a long *shooosh* and then a *whump* as the mortar exploded dead center in the truck, killing the four roadrats aboard it, destroying the vehicle, and putting the tortured prisoner out of his misery.

The militia cheered. And then fell silent as the four motorcycles leading the Horde, a mixture of roadrats and bikers, switched on their bikes' headlights. The headlights had been painted to resemble red, demonic eyes. Red eyes glowing against the night, tilted up so they seemed to be looking at the men along the tops of the wall.

Traveler checked through the binoculars again. Recognizing the potential of the mortar, the Black Rider had prudently retired to the rear. Like any wise general.

At the front of the line was another pickup, something mounted on the bed in its rear. A rocket-grenade launcher. Another of Frayling's party favors.

Traveler shouted orders. "Get the gate reinforced with anything around. Back a truck up to it, if you've got one. Anything big to block it. And then clear away; stand off about twenty feet—" He was interrupted by the arrival of the machine guns. Two of them. One of them, it was clear, was not in working order. There was a box of ammo for the functional gun. "Any of you men trained to use one of these?"

They looked at him dumbly.

Pearlman shrugged. "I'll do it."

"Okay. Set it up about forty feet inside the gate, behind whatever you can find for a bunker. They're about to blast that gate, unless we can take 'em out with the mortar. So far, they're out of range—no, here they come."

The mass of maniacs, like a single entity with four demonic red eyes, was moving across the flatlands, picking up speed as it approached the gate. Traveler loaded the mortar and tried to aim it at the onrushing truck. But a mortar isn't made for a moving target. He launched the rocket, and it fell a few yards behind the target, blasting an old GMC to pieces and the three men inside it to smaller pieces. The grenade-launching truck stopped, the men in its rear took aim—at the same moment as Travel hastily readjusted the mortar on the wall—and fired. Traveler fired a second later.

There were two explosions, one after the other. The rocket-grenade struck the city gate. And Traveler had scored a direct hit on the grenade launcher—the truck was exploding, enwrapped in eagerly burning flames. But there were screams from the courtyard below. Someone had been too close to the gate. Traveler moved to the stairway and looked down at the courtyard. The big metal gate was sagging inward, one of its hinges broken off. There was a roar as roadrats leaped from their vehicles to try to climb through the breach in the gate. The machine gun rattled, and the roadrats fell back, shot apart. A roadrat semi, its front end reinforced with

138

battering rams of layered wood and steel, ran at the gate, blasting its horn and rumbling.

Traveler ran to a battlement and snatched up the AR-180, aiming at the oncoming semi-truck. It was just twenty yards away. He drew a bead on the driver, who was howling with laughter, and squeezed the trigger. The laughter cut short, and the truck swerved, out of control, finally impacting with the wall beside the gate.

"Dump the oil on it!" Traveler shouted.

The men manning the steaming cauldron on the next battlement over tilted the cauldron on its swing-shaft, pouring burning petroleum on the semi and the roadrats trying to restart it. Howls of agony echoed through the night, and the truck caught fire, beginning to burn like some primeval beast caught in a lava flow. The flame reached the gas tank, and it exploded, sending shrapnel through the ranks of men trying to force the gate back.

The gate had been blocked by the city's only armored vehicle, salvaged from some deserted National Guard armory—a jeep with a heavy machine gun mounted in the back.

Traveler shouted orders to get the gate blocked with steel beams, which would be levered against the base of the tower across the courtyard. He had seen the big metal I-beams in a construction site a few blocks away. Men ran to follow his orders, commandeering one of the city's few working mobile cranes to bring the I-beams into position.

"I need the other mortars!" he shouted. The man who'd brought the first ran puffing up to him.

"Lord Vorsoon sends his compliments, sir—"

"Just get on with it!" Traveler barked.

"We have no more mortars, sir! The other one is missing! The sergeant at arms thinks the corporal sold it for—"

"Forget it! Get with the archers and do some killing!"

The man ran to the archers, who were sending volleys of arrows into the ranks of the roadrats, cutting some of them down.

Some of the bikers still carried grenades. They rode past the wall and used whirling slings to lob grenades onto the battlements. A flash and a thud, men screaming, falling. The archers began to run from their post. Traveler sighed.

He didn't like having to be a managerial type.

He ran to block off their rout and fired the HK91 in the air to get their attention. The archers, a score of them, stopped and stared. One of them pointed his crossbow at Traveler, and Traveler promptly shot him down.

"Any other deserters?" Traveler asked loudly.

The men looked at one another.

Traveler started yelling. "Is this your city or not? Where will you go if those assholes take it over? What will be left for you?"

The men seemed uncertain, wavering. One of them said, "It's hopeless! They have bombs!"

The word *bomb* was a word carrying a freight of great terror in the postwar world.

Just then, a squadron of hastily enlisted serfs ran up the stairs, newly assigned crossbows in hand. One of them, seeing somehow that Traveler was in authority, asked him, "Where do we go, sir?"

He was a boy, really.

"There are *bombs*, kid," Traveler said. "You going to run when the bombs fall?"

"We heard the explosions, sir," the boy said, shrugging. "We know what they mean. This place, though—it's all we've got."

The regular archers looked at one another sheepishly, and then at Traveler's HK. Dual influences—fear of Traveler and simple shame—made them turn and go back to their posts.

"You!" Traveler said, pointing at one of the regular archers. "Assign these new men positions and show 'em how to shoot the damn bows!"

Traveler turned away, wanting badly to be away from this place. It wasn't natural for him to be here. All these people—

A grenade arced over the wall and dropped toward his head. Almost absentmindedly he stepped back and, swinging the rifle like a baseball bat, holding it by its barrel, he whacked the grenade back over the wall with the rifle butt.

It fell into the wave of roadrats running at the gate . . . and exploded among them. The archers cheered, their morale improving. Traveler improved their morale twice more when he fired the mortar over the wall, taking out clumps of roadrats below.

There was a bullhorn shout, "Regroup, you scum!"

The roadrats and bikers retreated, reassembling their mass.

They'd taken heavy losses. But they'd also almost breached the gate, and they knew it. Still, most roadrats were not militarily disciplined and resented authority. They'd probably already begun peeling off, deserting.

He could, just possibly, disintegrate the roadrat army by taking from it the one thing that held it together.

He had run out of mortar shells, anyway.

He ran down the stairs to the courtyard. The I-beams were almost in place. Vorsoon was arguing with Pearlman.

"But it's only right that I have a turn on the machine gun!" Vorsoon was saying. "I know how to operate—"

"I was told to take orders from Traveler," Pearlman said, shrugging.

"You know how to operate this thing?" Traveler asked, looking at Vorsoon with a new depth of contempt. The guy thought the gun was a fucking toy.

"But of course I do!" Vorsoon blustered. "I was a captain in the reserves before—"

"Okay, okay. Take it up to the battlements, try to keep them away from the gate. There's only one crate of ammo, so be careful to use only what you need."

Pearlman stood up. "And me?"

"You're going with me . . . if you want to. It's no order. I'm taking that jeep . . . and going outside."

Pearlman shrugged. "I'm paid to be a damn fool. Let's get on with it."

The secret gate at the far side of the city was just big enough to let the jeep through. Pearlman was at the machine gun—with only two boxes of ammo—and Traveler was at the wheel. Pearlman carried the Armalite as backup; Traveler had the shotgun beside him, fully reloaded, and the forty-five.

Both of them were dressed in roadrat regalia taken from the bodies of the enemy who'd gotten inside the gate.

It was dark outside, and their faces were painted; they just might pass. The gate opened, and they shot through and into the night. At first the scrubland outside the gate seemed deserted, and then they drove through a roadrats' camp.

Pearlman shouted, "Look what we ripped offa the city! We gonna take it to the Black Rider!"

The roadrats whooped in approval and let them pass. Traveler smiled and drove on.

They followed a rutted road that circled the city's outer wall, swerving now and then to avoid open garbage pits. A family of squatters, denied residency in the city for obscure bureaucratic reasons, was picking through a garbage heap. They fled when the jeep whizzed past.

The jeep passed through two more roadrat "checkpoints"—the discipline, as Traveler had expected, was lax. They passed with no problem except suspicious stares.

"Maybe they outnumber us," Pearlman shouted to him when they'd gone through, "but we outbrain 'em. They're *dumb*."

But Traveler was thinking: *Not all of them are stupid.*

The Black Rider was a beacon of feral intelligence.

They had driven through the rubble of the ruins to one side of the Horde encampment. They came to another checkpoint at the edge of the camp, blocked off by cars and wooden roadblocks.

"Hey look what we stole—" Pearlman began.

"Who the fuck are *you*?" said a roadrat captain suspiciously. He wasn't buying the disguises. He was a fat man in a green coat. He had a patch over one eye; the surviving eye made him look like a predatory parrot.

"Show 'em who we are," Traveler shouted to Pearlman.

"Well, who we are," Pearlman said, swiveling the big gun around, "is—" He finished the sentence with machine gun bursts, chopping through the four men manning the barrier. He shot out the fat guy's remaining eye, and then Traveler floored it, and they smashed through the wooden barrier, boards flying to either side. They weaved in and out of campfires, cars, gunmen—grotesque faces looming up suddenly in the darkness like Halloween masks. Pearlman kept low, holding off on the gun.

They were just a thundering blur for the roadrats they passed. No one, except those left well behind, were sure whether they were friend or foe.

It would take awhile for word to get to the Black Rider from their entry point.

And then Traveler saw the black tent up ahead. He slowed and shouted over his shoulder, "I think that's it!" He reached for the coil of rope on the seat beside him.

The Black Rider was sitting in his tent on a camp chair, looking at the maps of Kansas City provided by Frayling's spies. Squid was looking over his master's shoulder.

"Here," the Black Rider said tonelessly. "We can send a squad in through these sewers. They can open the back gate—"

He broke off and looked up, frowning. An electric flicker showed in his onyx eyes.

"He's coming," the Black Rider said. There was an edge to his voice now. "He's near. *Near.*"

Squid straightened up and reached for his M16. "Who, Rider?"

"The one called—" He broke off and bolted through the door of the tent to his bike. Squid followed him through the flaps, then stared in puzzlement.

"Where you going?"

"Tell the other fools to wake up and look around! They're—"

There was a roar and the blinding approach of headlights; then Squid saw two roadrats returning fire from a man on the back of a jeep with the biggest goddamn machine gun he'd ever seen.

Squid dove for cover.

He dove into the tent—and the jeep ran right over it, breaking his back.

Traveler was only dimly aware of the screams from the man under the jeep. He pulled up short and grabbed the rope. He knew that the confusion of the roadrats around them wouldn't work to his advantage for long. It would turn to panic and anger and wild gunplay.

He put the jeep in idle and jumped out, running after the Black Rider, who was trying to ride out between a couple of pickup trucks. "Get out of the way, you fools!" the Rider shouted as a group of roadrats clustered in his way.

And then the noose at the end of Traveler's rope looped over the Black Rider's neck, pulled taut, and jerked him from his saddle.

Pearlman was working the machine gun, mowing down an onslaught of snarling road-maniacs. He cut down an oncoming hawg so it exploded, blowing its rider into three pieces.

The Black Rider snarled and struggled like a panther fighting a leash. Then, he turned toward Traveler, who had hitched the rope to the rear of the jeep. The Black Rider gathered his legs beneath him and sprang into the air.

He sprang at Traveler's back.

Traveler turned and saw the Black Rider coming down at him. For a moment it seemed as if the Black Rider were suspended in midair, arms and legs outspread, like a cat coming down, claws ready.

The Black Rider had leapt twenty feet straight up in the air and he was coming down at Traveler and his hands were outstretched and all Traveler could do was stand there looking up with a kind of awe. And Traveler said, "Jesus fucking Chr—"

He didn't have the chance to finish saying it.

14

Eye to Eye with Himself—and Tooth to Tooth

And then Traveler found himself on his back, with the spitting, white-toothed blackness clawing at him. The flash of a lifted knife. A black hand at his throat.

Traveler snapped out of his daze. His reflexes took charge, and his right hand shot out to grab the Black Rider's knifehand.

He found himself losing ground against a wiry, implacable strength that seemed to spring from icy places underground. He looked into the black, infinitely empty orbs of the Rider's eyes and felt himself losing all hope. Those eyes sucked the hope from him.

He summoned revolt from deep inside himself and built a fire against the darkness in the Black Rider's eyes, and the fire passed into Traveler's arms and somehow gave him the strength to twist, and wrench, and force the Black Rider over, until it was Traveler who was on top, banging the night-bound mutant's head onto the rocky ground.

After a moment the mutant's knifehand went limp, the dark eyes glazed. But Traveler knew the Rider was only stunned.

And he knew something else—the Black Rider scared him. He scared him because he recognized something of himself in this monster. Every man has a diabolic side—and Traveler's life had brought his own diabolic side nearly to the forefront. Sometimes, when he was caught up in a good fight, it seemed to take control of him. And that was scary.

He looked up . . . and saw a ring of roadrats closing in on the jeep.

But he lifted the Black Rider onto his shoulders and carried him into the jeep; then he held the knife to the Black Rider's throat and shouted, "Anybody gets any closer, we off your boss!"

He started the jeep and drove it one-handedly. Now and then a burst from Pearlman on the back of the jeep drove the roadrats back. "We've got the Black Rider, so don't fuck with us!" Pearlman shouted.

The roadrats, for the most part, seemed numbed. As if some mental control the Black Rider had had over them had faded when he'd lost consciousness—and now they were lost, a pack of wild dogs whose leader has vanished.

They drove unmolested out through the barrier, and Traveler picked up speed, heading back to the secret gate.

They paused in the darkness outside the gate. Traveler hoped the men who were supposed to be watching for him on the wall were really there. He flashed his headlights in the prearranged code. Pulleys creaked, wheels turned—the gate, hidden in a stone wall, opened, looking like piece of the wall swinging out.

He began to shift gears, in preparation for driving

through . . . and then he had a strange feeling. A kind of paralysis of the will.

He couldn't move.

Pearlman brought him out of it. "Traveler, damn it, let's move! There're roadrats coming!"

Traveler shook himself, then looked down at the floor where he'd left the unconscious Black Rider.

The Black Rider's eyes were open, staring at him—electric flickerings showing in them, the lips moving soundlessly. In the darkness of the jeep's interior the Black Rider was almost invisible; he seemed to have flowed into the shadows. Only the lineaments of his face, the onyx gleam, and electric crackle of his eyes were visible.

Traveler felt a long, low shudder of horror.

He could feel the Black Rider's will begin to creep over his own again.

A fury of rebellion came over him. "Pearlman!" he shouted. "Help me, dammit!"

The Black Rider flung himself at Traveler, his teeth gnashing for Traveler's throat.

Traveler struck at him, feeling strangely weak, as if, as happens in nightmares, his limbs had gone all rubbery, empty of bone, pulled apart. Out of some distant childhood memory he seemed to hear: "Noooooooo, Mr. Bill!"

Then Pearlman had the Black Rider by the throat, was dragging him back. Pearlman was big, and the Rider had been taken by surprise. Pearlman yanked on the rope still noosed around the Black Rider's throat. The black mutant gagged and writhed, once more a leashed wild panther.

Pearlman threw the mutant on the ground, took up part of the slack on the rope, and shouted, "Drive!"

149

Traveler came awake, the dream that wasn't a dream fading. He put the jeep in gear, heard a shriek of animal rage from the Rider, and drove through the gate. The mutant was dragged by the rope, preventing himself from being choked only by gripping the noose hard with his night-colored hands. He was dragging behind like a fishing lure, turning, twisting, bouncing on the road, four feet back of the jeep, the earth itself gnawing at him, ripping away the black leather, shredding his skin.

And then they'd passed through the gate.

It closed behind them, and for a moment Traveler thought the Black Rider had been crushed in it. Until he heard him moan.

Pearlman said, "Wait here," and went back to truss the thing up. They called for guards, who carried the half-conscious, bloodied mutant to a cell.

Vorsoon met them there as they locked the door on the Rider.

"That is their . . . leader?" he asked, running his fingers through his beard.

"Yeah, and I think you ought to take him and hang him," Traveler said. "Where the Horde out there can see him. Let them see him swing and then open fire on them and they'll probably disperse."

"Hang him? But if as you say he is working with Frayling, he is valuable to us! We must interrogate him! It could take a long time, but we will make him talk."

Traveler shook his head. "Don't let him live. Kill him quick."

Pearlman looked at Traveler, frowning. "What's the

hurry, now or in a few days? They can show him to the mob, hang him by his ankles."

Traveler shook his head more emphatically.

"Kill him" was all he said. "Kill him if you're smart." And he walked away.

But they didn't do it. They wasted time arguing about what they should do, and in the meantime, the Black Rider came to himself in the cell. He flexed his muscles, and concentrated, and the ropes slid off of him. They seemed to crawl off, as if repelled by him—and they had been.

Pearlman had gone to find Traveler. Vorsoon had gone to the baron to discuss the matter with him.

There was only a young guard outside the door, and he had no idea what he was guarding.

But the word had already spread through the Horde. *They've got the Black Rider!*

The Horde milled, confused, directionless, as three or four roadrat captains vied for control. Others deserted, wondering why they'd joined in the first place, vaguely aware that the Rider had once had some kind of strange hold over them.

Traveler looked over the wall and saw the moment had come.

A half hour later the secret gate opened again, and the jeep emerged, driven by Pearlman, followed by trucks containing two thirds of the city's remaining militia and volunteers. Every automatic weapon available was out front in the column. And someone had produced an M79 and four black-market high-explosive rounds. Traveler took charge of these. Just after midnight they broke into two forks and cut into the mass of the Horde from the northeast and southeast, coming on with weapons blazing, volleys of arrows falling.

Traveler rode the Meat Wagon at the head of the southeast contingent. He'd replenished the drums on the twin K21's and used them to cut a deep swathe through the ranks of the roadrats. Pinchello rode beside him and on Traveler's order fired the grenade launcher through the side window.

It was a trick.

The whole assault was a trick. Because the Kansas City forces were outnumbered three to one. And they were using up their gun ammo rapidly. In a few minutes they'd be reduced to arrows and pikes and knives. But Traveler was gambling on the roadrats' rootlessness, their lack of direction without a definite leader present, their disdain for belonging to so big a social machine as an army. Their panic.

The panic came first. The rout was almost a complete success. The army split up, roadrats running off in bunches in this direction and that, with no sense of strategic retreat, like a mass of cockroaches frightened by a light in the kitchen.

But the Motorcycle Madmen who'd followed the Black Rider, his particular people, were more reluctant to run. Maybe they felt he was still alive, in there. Maybe they seemed to hear him say, "Fight on, kill them, don't run, break through. . . ."

They stayed together, regrouped, and coming on in a flying V, rode hard at Traveler's column.

Pearlman and Traveler had rendezvoused in the midst of the battleground. Pearlman, looking annoyed, like a PE teacher breaking up a fight in the schoolyard, climbed out of the jeep and took up the gunnery post at the replenished machine gun. He stood behind the gun, both hands on its throttles, and swung it to meet the oncoming flying V of heavy-metal thunder.

Traveler backed up, then swung in a circle around the approaching force, hitting them from the flank as Pearlman gunned them down at their point. Traveler switched off his headlights. The dark van was almost lost in the darkness.

Traveler stepped hard on the gas and waited till the MCs—red-lit silhouettes and metal gleam, the occasional flash of a grinning face—came into his firing zone.

It was hard to see, though some parts of the battlefield were lit by lights from the city wall and from the red-edged glow of the burning cars lashing flame here and there and the bonfires and torches of the enemy mob.

And then the Meat Wagon was almost on top of the line of bikes. Two of them saw him coming, the Meat Wagon suddenly seeming to materialize out of the night, guns blazing atop, the *whooof* of a grenade launcher at its side window. Those two bikers saw that much, and that's the last they ever saw, as machine gun rounds kicked them off their bikes, and they went spinning into eternal night.

Traveler swerved to avoid collision with other bikes, and the van rocked with the shock wave of an explosion as Pinchello, cackling like a schoolboy shooting at birds with a slingshot, blew four bikers away with a well-placed grenade.

They'd cut through one wing of the V; now they were coming to the other, the end four of that formation.

Traveler cut down two with the topside MGs, knocking them down like shooting gallery targets whizzing by. The last two he scotched with the simple expedient of ramming, hitting the nearest with a rhinoceros-slam at an angle—so it didn't damage the van badly—and sending the biker and his bike spinning end over end backward into his compadre. The bikes collided in midair and interlocked their twisting steel, the flesh of their riders mixed in with that torn metal to become forever a part of the machines they'd revered.

Traveler cut a sharp left and swung across the darkened battlefield back toward Pearlman. He switched on his headlight, and in it saw that Pearlman was surrounded by four bikers.

The machine gun on the jeep was near the end of its belt, and Pearlman had no time to reload. A big, scarfaced biker with a cy-sick whirling in his hand leapt off his bike and onto the jeep's MG platform and whipped the whirling scythe into Pearlman's gut. Pearlman grunted and stumbled back, then seemed to gather strength. He jerked the machine gun around on its tripod and shoved the muzzle into the biker's belly, squeezing the trigger.

The expression "he blew him away" was never so apt.

The biker seemed to explode like an overblown balloon, red stuff flying to spatter everything within ten feet.

Then another biker swung a shotgun at Pearlman and let go a double-barreled blast. Pearlman was caught in the throat, his head severed from his neck. For a moment his body remained standing, headless, and in its death-twitchings his fingers squeezed off the last few rounds of the machine-gun belt, taking vengeance on the biker who'd shot him, cutting him in two at the waist. . . . Pearlman's body then fell forward over the MG, was propped up by it. . . .

And gave rise to a legend that was to grow in stature among bikers for years afterwards. *Then, see, the headless body just stood there and kept shootin' and shootin', laughter was comin' out of the hole where his neck was shot open and—*

Traveler came roaring out of the night, the van's MGs spitting fire. He blew the wheels out from under one bike. The biker leapt off and climbed onto the back of his compadre's machine, shouting in his ear, "Fuck the Black Rider! These assholes aren't human!"

They got out of there fast.

And the rout was complete.

Pinchello led Traveler up the steep stairs to his room. "It's here, Cat-Loved Lord of the Black Van, Sir Traveler sir," Pinchello said, practically dancing with his happiness. They had won the battle, driven the roadrats away, and he, Pinchello, had ridden beside the general who'd come as the Cat Rider had prophesied, and no more would the ladies of the court refuse his attentions!

Traveler, however, was feeling like a lump of animated lead.

He was dog-tired and disgusted. He'd been sorry to see Pearlman die.

All he wanted now was a night's sleep and to get out of this town. After he collected his fee.

There were footsteps in the corridor. Sandy and a man Traveler didn't recognize came around the corner. The man wore an old-fashioned three-piece suit; but on his head, looking ridiculous with the suit, was a sort of stylized knight's helmet, its visor open. He was an attractive, soft-looking young man with a manicure. Very clean.

Sandy was wearing a long, flowing blue dress and a tall peaked hat trailing a scarf. She was made up and pristine like a fairy-tale princess, and looking at her now, Traveler could hardly believe some of the things he had done with her in the Meat Wagon.

Traveler was suddenly conscious that he was caked with blood and dirt and had a five-days growth of beard. The young man raised an eyebrow, looking at him.

"Traveler," said Sandy, rather formally, "this is Baron Moorcock's son, Frank Moorcock."

"*Frank?*" Traveler said. "Jesus."

Moorcock, apparently resigned to soiling his hands, reached out to shake. "Mr. Traveler, Frank Moorcock!"

Traveler stared at the hand. "I'm too tired for rituals."

"Ah." Moorcock dropped the hand but managed to seem unsnubbed. He beamed. "Well, I'll *bet* you're tired! I've heard those people have been completely dispersed. And you captured their leader! My father is going to declare a feast in your honor!"

"Great," said Traveler, with heavy irony.

Moorcock didn't catch the irony. "Maybe we could combine your feast with our wedding feast! Say, that would save us a packet!"

"Frank's the city's accountant," Sandy said a bit wearily.

"*Treasurer*, my dear, *treasurer!*" Moorcock said, with mock reproach. "Well . . . we just wanted to congratulate you, Traveler. So—"

"I want my pay first thing in the morning. Sandy knows what it is. Ammo, gasoline or some other high-grade fuel, the gold, and food. So you see to that, Treasurer."

He turned to the door. All this time Pinchello had been standing by silently, looking with awe at each of them. He hastily opened the door for Traveler, then said, "Good night, General Traveler sir!"

Traveler went into the room and, with a relieved sigh, closed the door behind him.

In the hall Pinchello saluted the treasurer, who ignored him.

"Rude sort of man, this Traveler," Moorcock was saying.

There was a hot bath waiting for him in his chamber. Traveler had to grudgingly admit that somebody around here had it on the ball. He stripped and got in, letting himself relax. It was a big ceramic tub right in the middle of the bedroom, filled with soapy hot water. There was a towel, clean and dry, folded over a chair beside the bath.

It felt great.

He was almost asleep when he heard a light footstep behind him. Then he saw the flash of a blade from the corner of his eye.

He turned and caught the wrist of the hand holding the blade. It was a slim white wrist.

"Sandy!" he blurted. "What the fuck you doing?"

"Let my arm go, you ape! That hurts!"

"What's with the—oh." He saw the shaving mug in her other hand. And the blade in her free hand was a straight razor. He let go and turned to sink back into the bath. "Sorry."

"I guess I shouldn't have snuck up on you like that. I wanted it to be a surprise. My room adjoins yours." She giggled. "I made the room assignments myself. Frank doesn't know."

"Frank." He closed his eyes. "Frank."

She lathered him and, quite expertly, shaved him. "I used to do this for my dad." She finished and wiped the lather away.

Then he heard a whisper of cloth as she removed her lingerie. She climbed into the tub with him.

"What the hell do you think you're doing?" he asked, trying to be cold with her.

"Tough guy," she said, and pressed her big, soapy breasts against him. His erection sprang up to meet them, and she began to work it back and forth between those breasts, hot and slippery and sweet, and he bent, found her lips—and they were hot and slippery and sweet too.

"If I were you, Mortner," Vorsoon was saying lightly, "I'd stay well out of sight. Traveler has been asking for you. And I *don't* think he wants to have tea with you."

"It's a crime," Mortner complained, his froggish mouth turning down at the ends, "that the baron should honor that man! He nearly ran off with the princess, he struck me down—me, a representative of the Kingdom of Wichita!"

They were standing on the street, that sunny morning, in the shadow of the bridge beside the Baron's Towers.

Just above them, crouching in the damp, dark place atop a stone column, where there was a ledge beside the join with the bridge overhead, were Merle and Ugly Bro. They were achingly tired and cold, having spent the night there. But Ugly Bro was trying to hear what the men below him were saying. He'd heard

Traveler and *Kingdom of Wichita*. He'd learned all about that, listening here and there around the city, the night before. Traveler was the one they sought. But they hadn't seem him or the girl. They knew that Traveler must be in the tower, however. And they knew that Mortner was connected with Traveler— therefore he must be one of Traveler's comrades.

And they had something special with them. It was a lovely little bomb—as Ugly Bro described it—which they'd stolen from a heap of armaments being loaded onto a truck during the confusion of the siege on the city. It was an oval bomb with a timer on it. Ugly Bro thought it looked big enough—it was big as a fair-sized watermelon—to cause the nearest tower of the Baron's Towers to fall.

That'd bring the whole castle down on Traveler and that bitch who'd stabbed Ugly Bro in the face.

Since this man Mortner was with Traveler, they'd get him too. Now. No one was around. Mortner and Vorsoon were strolling away side by side.

Merle and Ugly Bro lowered the big gray oval of the bomb to the empty side street in a rope sling. They tied the rope around the column and lowered themselves down it. That was painful for Merle—he was still hurting from his wound.

There was a niche in the wall of the Towers, across the street, where sometimes a guard stood. But he wasn't there now. He was dead on the battlefield. Another hadn't yet been assigned. The city was confused and understaffed.

About twenty yards to Ugly Bro's left a market was beginning to bustle. Serfs were arranging rows of vegetables. The serfs were bleary from the victory feast

159

that had taken place in their simple quarters the night before.

No one was looking.

Ugly Bro picked up the bomb and looked again at its knobs and dials. It was actually a high-powered land mine, made to blow up a large armored vehicle. It was supposed to be command-detonated, set off by a radio signal. But the radio had been lost or destroyed years ago, and someone had installed a crude timer. Ugly Bro thought the numbers on its dial, from one to sixty, represented minutes. They stood for seconds. The bomber was supposed to bury the bomb, except for its knob, set it for one minute, and run like hell, presumably just before an armored vehicle came around the bend.

It was a stupid, obsolete weapon, which was why it ended up in the Kansas City armory.

Ugly Bro gave it to Merle and said, "Here, take it across the street and put it in that hole inna wall where the guard's supposed to stand. Set it for one minute."

Ugly Bro didn't want to be seen on the street. He didn't mind risking Merle. Ugly Bro stepped behind a column.

Merle set the bomb for what he thought was a one-minute detonation. But it was for one second. Actually, it took four seconds to detonate, not being made very well, so he took two strides and then—

—was vaporized in a ball of flame that reached up to smack the underside of the bridge with terrific force.

The bridge buckled and began to collapse.

Mortner, down the street just twelve yards, panicked, seeing the bridge beginning to fall, and in his confusion ran the wrong way. Vorsoon ran for the safety of the Towers.

Mortner and Ugly Bro ran right into each other. And then the bridge fell atop them.

"*Now* what?" Sandy said, feeling the explosion shiver through the building. She sat up in bed beside Traveler.

Traveler stretched lazily. "Probably a revolution. Some of your serfs getting smart."

She turned to look hard at him, swallowing. She'd read about Marie Antoinette. "Do you really think so?"

"No. I think some jerk was careless with some of those explosives. They were piling them in the street last night like pumpkins. I told 'em . . ." He shrugged, got up, and went naked to the window. Two stories below he saw the smoking wreckage of the collapsed bridge. Faintly, he heard someone screaming from inside the rubble.

He scratched himself and yawned.

He heard Vorsoon shouting, "Some fool . . . careless . . ."

"That's what I thought," Traveler said. He went back to bed.

"Traveler . . ." Sandy said, running her hands up and down him. "We can still get out. We can slip out of the city and . . . I mean, this guy Frank's not bad. In some ways."

"Yeah. So what if he's an accountant. Maybe he's a *wild man* in bed." Traveler laughed.

"You're avoiding the subject."

Traveler sat up. He shrugged irritably and went to the chamber's refrigerator. He took out the vial of serum, swallowed some, and made a face. He replaced it and went to get into his clothes. To his amazement someone had cleaned them.

161

"Where are you going?" she asked.

"To see if my van's being repaired and loaded with the stuff they promised me."

"It is—Frank promised *me*. Look, how about if I slip out the back gate and you pick me up—"

"Uh-uh."

She sat up, her breasts bouncing with the movement. Her eyes couldn't decide about their expression. One moment they were filling with tears, the eyes of a hurt little girl, the next they were hard and angry, the eyes of a woman scorned . . . then they got the hurt child look again.

He stopped looking at her.

"What are you doing?" she said. "Playing the Rambling Man? The tough wanderer who needs no one? It's bullshit!"

"I'm not playing anything. I'm dead serious. I'm going to find a certain guy, if he's alive, and kill him. His name is Vallone. Last night Vorsoon was interrogating roadrat prisoners. He told me one of them said that a Major Vallone was working with the Black Rider. It's the guy I'm looking for; the description fit the name. And I don't expect to come out of it in one piece, and it's simple as that."

"Look, why waste your life chasing some asshole—"

"And there's another thing." The tone of his voice cut her off. He went on, "This shit-hole of a city needs you. These people need civilization. You can take a hand in it. Have a dozen boyfriends on the side, but stay here and get this place into shape. You can become influential . . . and eventually force 'em to have an election. Otherwise—" he shrugged. "These people are going to revolt. . . ."

162

He went to the door. He stopped and turned to her, saying, "Look, I'm crazy about you, but this is the end of it. Your people need you, and I need to get the hell away. But . . . I figure we'll probably see each other again, sometime."

He went into the hall and found Pinchello waiting for him.

"The dark army of shit-heads are all gone, sir," said Pinchello. "But . . ."

"But what?"

"So is this Black Rider. He . . . he did something to the mind of the man guarding the cell. He got away, and he found that motorbicycle machine. We had it locked up. But he found it, and someone saw him ride away from the city."

Traveler swore. He knew he had a long-term enemy in the Black Rider.

Pinchello asked, "Do you think he'll bring the armies back?"

"What? No. They're dispersed. And Frayling won't help him anymore. By now the city's sent a message to Frayling telling him they're on to him. No, but that mutant . . ."

He shook his head and clapped Pinchello on the shoulders. "Is my van ready, Pinchello?"

"Yes, O Great—"

"I told you to can that stuff. Is everything I asked for in the van?"

"Yes, sir."

"Then I'm going, man. Heading, I think, for Las Vegas. See you later. Some year."

"But, General Traveler—"

163

"Oh, one thing. . . ." Traveler's fists clenched. "Have you seen that asshole Mortner?"

"The man from Wichita? They say he was caught in the bridge collapse."

Traveler was disappointed. He'd liked to have gotten his hands on the son-of-a-bitch.

Mortner was alive.

He was trapped under two large pieces of masonry that leaned together, forming a sort of angular arch over him. Other chunks of stone held him down, flat on his back. One of his legs was smashed, but he was otherwise intact. A little light came from a small hole in the masonry overhead, a dust-filled yellow ray that fell on the face of the man lying beside Mortner. A hideous, disfigured face, without lips.

The man was Ugly Bro.

He was trapped under the rubble, too, but he had one arm free, and unbroken. And he had a large sharp stone in the hand of that arm, a stone rather like a flint knife, which he'd found in the rubble.

"You," Ugly Bro said, looking at Mortner.

Mortner whimpered.

"You," Ugly Bro repeated.

Mortner looked away.

"I am broken and dying," Ugly Bro said. "I will be dead soon. But you are the friend of that Traveler. I heard that. You came with him. You will suffer for him, because I cannot reach him. And you are his friend, so you will be real happy to suffer for this man. Right?"

"No!" Mortner moaned. "I—" He couldn't say anything else because the monster had stuffed a handful of gravel into his mouth. And a fist-sized rock. He could hardly breathe.

"It will be hours," said Ugly Bro, his breathing raspy, "before they get you dug out of here. When they find you, they will wish they hadn't taken the trouble."

Then he began to use the flint knife on Mortner's face.

The open road. Plenty of fuel and food and ammo.

There was an ache in him, but he ignored it, and it'd go away. He'd keep himself busy. He had a lot of traveling to do.

Traveler pushed a cassette tape into the player in his dashboard. It was one of three tapes he'd found, recently, in an old wreck. The cassette deck blasted an old song by the Doors: "Keep your eyes on the road and your hands upon the wheel . . ." Jim Morrison sang.

"Yeah, Jim," Traveler muttered.

He stepped on the accelerator. He floored it.

Fifteen years after the bombs dropped the man called Traveler had only two goals—to keep moving and to stay alive. He'd been doing fine until he met

THE STALKERS

Traveler #3

by D. B. Drumm

1

The Bloats

He moved across the land like a ricocheting bullet.

Traveler drove the Meat Wagon, the sleek black armored van, across the post-holocaust wastelands of the Southwestern United States at top speed, almost always in a straight line—till he came to an obstacle. And then he crashed through it or rebounded from it. Like a ricocheting bullet, leaving something smashed where he'd struck . . . and speeding onward.

And he knew that sooner or later a ricocheting bullet runs out of momentum. Ends up buried in the earth, flattened.

But there was no use thinking about that. When your number's up, it's up.

It was a hot June day in what had once been central Nevada. There was no Nevada anymore, because there was no state government. They were all dead.

Most of the nation had died, fifteen years before, in the nuclear holocaust that had pretty much put an end to civilized life in the Northern Hemisphere.

The roads were still there—some of them. Cracked, fissured, interrupted, but still pulsing with traffic. The pulses, to be sure, came like the pulse of a dying man. In fits, trailing out. But now and then there was life, of a sort. A scrofulous, hungry, crazed sort, most of it, like the roadrats, the madmen who lived nomadically along the roads, resembling Indians gone punk, heavy-metal savages preying on those who tried to survive in the few tiny clots of semicivilized order remaining. Torturing, brutalizing, trying to project the horror that had eaten up their own sanity onto the world around them. And there were other things, worse things, stalking the road . . .

As Traveler was about to find out.

Traveler stopped the van in the middle of the road. The long cape of yellow dust behind the Meat Wagon overtook it, and billowed like a djinn overhead as he climbed out of the cab, a 12-gauge pump in the crook of his arm.

He wasn't a tall man. Five nine, five ten, thereabouts. He was lean, and cat-limber, and strong with the strength of long endurance cut with burning inner intensity. His depthless blue eyes and rugged, weatherbeaten, strong-jawed face told you nothing about what was going on in his head. Unless he wanted you to know something. And even then, you might see only a flicker. But he had human feelings all right—locked up in him, in a steel safe that was his soul—in a safe to which he had long ago forgotten the combination.

Today he wore a flak-jacket—like the one he'd worn on Long Range Recon Patrol sorties, fighting in Central America two decades before—along with combat pants and boots. A black bandanna, tied like a headband, kept sweat and his spiky brown hair out of his eyes.

There was something wrong with the road up ahead. Something unusually wrong.

It was the way the cracks in it looked. Something screwy about their pattern. . . .

The asphalt highway was coated with dust from the yellowish, almost featureless desert to either side. But you could see the shape the road was in, through the dust, and Traveler had learned to read it like a tropics dweller reading the sky for signs of a monsoon, or a riverboater who watches the currents, who knows instinctively when the river is about to become dangerous.

The road was Traveler's home, his world, his medium. And it was trying to warn him.

Those cracks were new, and converging toward the center of the road. As if it had sagged—and then been lifted up again. As if someone had undermined the road and then reinforced it—from beneath.

He pumped a round into the chamber of the shotgun in his hands.

He could feel the gunmetal warming in the sunlight. It was as if the shotgun were coming to life.

The heavy pumpgun was loaded with double-ought buckshot. There was room for eight shells in the tube, but Traveler had only six left. Ammo was hard to come by in post-holocaust America. So hard to come by, it was used as an important trading currency. Traveler had a pretty good supply of ammo for his other guns. There was the AR15 in the weapons rack inside. The two convergently-trained 7.62 mm HK-21 machine guns mounted on the roof of the van were operated from within the cab by a push button he'd set up on his steering column. There was also a fully-loaded Colt .45 Mark IV pistol he carried as a backup in the holster under his jacket.

He scanned the flat horizon. Here and there it was broken by a twisted tree or an outcropping of rock. There was no movement.

But he could sense a trap.

He could feel them nearby. Something malevolent, and angry, and crippled up inside. The neurotoxin damage he'd sustained because of Vallone's treachery in that El Hiaguran jungle clearing had had an unforeseen side effect. It had made his senses, at times, almost supernaturally sharp. And it had awakened the animal's sixth sense, present in primeval man but long buried in most modern men—the proximity sense. The sense that feels another life energy nearby.

And now he sensed something—no, someone—beneath him.

"Shit," he muttered, getting back into the van. He tossed the shotgun into the passenger seat, threw the idling vehicle into gear, and backed up, fast.

A quick twenty-five feet, and he stopped the van and stared at the road.

It was buckling, falling like stretched dough, as someone beneath removed support beams. Ten, fifteen, twenty feet. Gone, a pit now. He'd pulled up, before, right on the edge of it.

The smart thing to do would be to U-turn, go back, and find another route. But it was a hundred miles back to the nearest alternate road. And he had business up ahead. Somewhere farther south was the underground military base occupied by what shreds remained of the U.S. Government. And somewhere in that hidden complex was Major Vallone.

Traveler wanted to have a few words with Vallone.

So he had to go on.

He swung right, into the desert, trying to cut across the wastelands, circle the ambush site, get back on the road.

But they were here too. There was a screen of waist-high boulders to his right—a flanking team of the ambushers had been waiting there, flattened, expecting him to make just this maneuver.

They leaped up now, and he had a blurry impression of them coming at him. He almost gagged.

They were mutants—what roadrats called Bloats. Swollen, misshapen bodies as distorted as shapes seen in funhouse mirrors, most of them some seven feet tall. Theoretically they were children—none older than fourteen. Children by human standards. But they weren't human. Like some deranged species of ape, they came to full maturity at nine years old. It was the extra holes in their heads that made them hard to look at—inch-wide holes like pointless nostrils scattered about the skull, each of the dozen holes always bubbling with pus and froth, or flickering with tiny little pink tongues. Their mouths were so wide they looked as if they went nearly all the way around with just a couple of inches unbroken at the back of the neck. Their eyes drooped unevenly, yellow-filmed and owl-round. Their hands were as big as shovels and equipped with long, horny fingers, each one wickedly taloned. They were cunning, and industrious when they wanted to be. And they were always hungry, and human flesh was the most abundant and easy prey for them.

They came at him with mouths open so wide, he thought their heads would fall apart—big gray tongues

173

vibrating as they yowled out their war cry, which sounded eerily like the air-raid sirens he'd heard just before the bombs came, fifteen years before. They were wearing nothing at all, their scarred, hairy hides hanging in folds over flapping genitals. Each one was carrying a club or a kind of homemade scythe constructed from jagged pieces of scrap metal lashed to splintery wood with strips of leather. One of these swished through his open side window and slashed at his left shoulder, raking the flesh just enough to leave an arc of blood. Steering with his left hand, he drew the .45 and fired it point-blank into the face of the Bloat angling the crude scythe for another slash. Its lump of a forehead exploded with red, and there was a thirteenth unnatural hole in its head. This one spewed brains as it fell back, sirening plaintively.

Traveler cut to the left, fishtailing over the sand, the four-wheel-drive Meat Wagon spitting grit in spumes behind its massive black wheels as it fought for ground. A dozen mutants clung to it, holding on to the roof, the door handles, the wedgelike snout up front; clawing at the windows; hacking and banging, so metal rang on metal and sparks flew.

He caught a whipping motion out of the corner of his eye and turned in time to see a ten-foot catapult snapping up to lob a bushel-sized boulder at him. The big yellow-gray boulder grew, seeming to come on in slow motion.

And then it struck the Meat Wagon's front end. The whole structure shuddered and the van jounced on its shocks—and ground to a halt.

The boulder had broken something in the engine.

Traveler lost his temper.

174

It wasn't so much that he was probably going to get himself snuffed now, and eaten raw by this walking debris. It was—*they'd screwed up his van!*

He shot a hole through the twisted wrist of a scaly hand reaching through the window—fragments of bone flew, blood spattered, and the thing squealed and jerked its useless hand back. At the same moment Traveler caught up the shotgun and fired it through the right-hand window, catching two Bloats in their stumpy yellow teeth. Gunsmoke filled the cab of the Meat Wagon as he pumped another round into the chamber and let go another ear-splitting shotgun roar through the left-hand window, at a range of one yard, taking a Bloat's head cleanly off its shoulders. The headless body staggered around, clawing at the air, an ugly meat-fountain of blood—and then fell away to be replaced by a half-dozen whole Bloats sirening their battle cry.

Traveler pumped his last round into the chamber, raised it to his shoulder, and squeezed the trigger. It was a hard position to be shooting from, the kick from the big shotgun jerking his shoulder unmercifully. The oncoming Bloats were about twenty feet away, whirling the scythes over their hideous heads. They looked like figures of candle wax that had been held too close to the flame. They shrieked as the spreading shotgun pellets lashed into them, putting out eyes and punching into throats.

He tossed the shotgun aside. Up ahead the contingent that had been hiding in some side-trench under the road had come out and were running at him in a squalid group of eight. He smiled as they came within the convergent-fire scope of his overhead MGs—he pressed the fire button on the steering column.

Nothing happened.

The boulder had knocked out the van's electrical system, which controlled the machine guns.

He scrambled into the back, reaching for the AR15. He heard a scream of pain to his left as a Bloat opened the van's rear door. Traveler had booby-trapped the door, using a spring-tension launcher, and the mutant staggered back with a ten-inch wooden spike through its blood-spurting throat.

Traveler had just got the AR15 down, primed and ready, when the next mutie came through the now unprotected rear door. He swung the rifle around and greeted his unwanted guest with a four-round burst that opened him up like a can of tomato soup. Another one—

But there were two more scrambling through the front.

He squeezed off two shots at the rear door, swung around, and had just time enough to squeeze the trigger once before the stone ax caught him on the side of the head and exploded the world into blue sparkle.

As he sank into unconsciousness, not expecting to wake again, he grasped at one last satisfaction: the son of a bitch who'd clubbed him was going down too, with a bullet between his animal eyes.